"Let's pretend I'm crying. What do you do?"

Jarred looked at Serena a good long time. Then, he folded his arms around her and held her close. Real close.

With supreme effort, she focused. Just when she was about to tell him that gentlemen did not grab their women and plaster them against their bodies, one of his hands patted her head...and then drifted to her back.

Then lower.

Then settled on her...rear end?

"There, there, honey. Stop crying, now," he crooned, patting her butt.

Even though she knew they were only pretending... Even though she knew he'd never thought of her as anything more than his pal...it was as if her body had never gotten that memo.

He let out a little groan as his hands readjusted themselves again, cupping her rear.

She knew she should stop him.

She knew she should tell him that it wasn't good manners to grab girls' rears. But she couldn't do it.

Her hands itched to move. To circle around his neck. To pull his head down and ~~~~~~~~~~~~~~~~~~~~ own.

Just for a second...

Dear Reader,

Welcome to the world of the Riddells! I do so hope you will enjoy getting to know the Riddell brothers, Jarred, Junior and Trent. Writing this trilogy has been such a wonderful experience for me. I got to pretend I was back in Texas, when weekends were spent at our ranch and February meant late nights at the Houston Livestock Show and Rodeo. Those were good times and were filled with wonderful memories of my father.

I'm smiling as I write this note, because, see, I have a secret. I'm allergic to horses. And hay. And cows. We're talking *really* allergic. So even though we did have horses on our ranch, I never rode them. Which means, I guess, that I was destined to *write* about cowboys and horses and rodeo stars—since I certainly couldn't participate too much at all.

If you, like me, only get the chance to dream about cowboys and such, I hope you'll stick with these Riddells for the whole series. These guys are adorable, rich and, well, just a little bit needy. They require strong women to keep them in line and show them how to love.

From the moment I wrote the first word of *My Favorite Cowboy*, I loved these Riddells. They made me smile. They made me sigh. And, just for a little while, they reminded me of being eighteen again. Dressed in too-tight Wranglers, wearing old boots on my feet…and looking forward to a new day in my beautiful, wonderful Lone Star State.

With all my best to you,

Shelley Galloway

My Favorite Cowboy

SHELLEY GALLOWAY

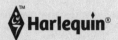

Harlequin®

TORONTO NEW YORK LONDON
AMSTERDAM PARIS SYDNEY HAMBURG
STOCKHOLM ATHENS TOKYO MILAN MADRID
PRAGUE WARSAW BUDAPEST AUCKLAND

Recycling programs
for this product may
not exist in your area.

ISBN-13: 978-0-373-75353-6

MY FAVORITE COWBOY

ABOUT THE AUTHOR

Shelley Galloway grew up in Houston, Texas, left for college in Colorado, then returned to Dallas for six years. After teaching lots and lots of sixth graders, she now lives with her husband, aging beagle and barking wiener dog in southern Ohio. She writes full-time. To date, Shelley has penned more than thirty novels for various publishers, both as Shelley Galloway for the Harlequin American Romance line, and as Shelley Shepard Gray for Avon Inspire.

Her novels have appeared on bestseller lists. She won a Reviewers' Choice Award in 2006 and a HOLT Medallion in 2009. Currently, she writes all day, texts her college son too much and tries not to think about her daughter going to college next year, too. Please visit her online at www.eharlequin.com or her website, www.shelleygalloway.com.

Books by Shelley Galloway

HARLEQUIN AMERICAN ROMANCE

1090—CINDERELLA CHRISTMAS
1134—SIMPLE GIFTS
1156—A SMALL-TOWN GIRL
1183—THE GOOD MOTHER
1212—THE MOMMY BRIDE
1244—MOMMY IN TRAINING
1291—BABY MAKES SIX
1312—SECOND CHANCE HERO

To Mendy. A wonderful woman,
a terrific Texan, and an amazing friend.
Thanks for all of your help and advice.
And laughter, too.

Chapter One

"Come on, Serena, don't be so cruel. You gotta help me or I won't never get the girl."

Serena Higgens focused on the crown of Jarred Riddell's straw hat. Far better to glare at that than the sunny smile he was directing her way. Even after all this time, that flash of teeth still managed to send a hundred little pulses of awareness through her.

Not that he needed to know that. "I don't have to help you with anything. And don't say 'won't never,' Jarred. It's a double negative."

In an instant, his eyes turned warm and languid and gorgeous. "See, that's *exactly* what I'm talking about. I need your help speaking more clearly. Without it, I'm gonna be in a heap of trouble." He winked conspiratorially as he struck a pose right out of *GQ Magazine,* leaning one hand up against a row of books in the library. "Fact is, I really do need to get auctioned off something awful."

Serena pretended she wasn't affected by his stance, his smile, his wink or by his very being.

That pretending didn't go too far, though. She hadn't been immune to Jarred Riddell's charms when she was fifteen and their dads used to do the rodeo circuit together. She didn't think it was very fair that he could still make her pulse jump at twenty-five. A girl ought to have come up with some kind of resistance in ten years.

"Honestly, Jarred. The things you think about."

"I'm not the only one. This auction's a big deal."

"I suppose…though I don't know why Electra even needs a community auction, anyway. It's demeaning, don't you think?"

"Not necessarily. Depends on whether the folks getting auctioned off have a problem with it."

"I think there's got to be a couple dozen better ways to add money to the Electra Community Fund."

"That may be, but I can't think of another idea that's half as fun." Focusing too-blue eyes right on her, he added, "You know as well as I do that the whole town is excited about next month's auction. As excited as all get-out."

"I wouldn't go that far." Though, she privately reflected, Jarred was pretty darn close. Every other conversation she heard seemed to be focused on who was going to be up for bid—and who wanted to do the bidding.

"I would. Don't be such a spoilsport. No one else is complaining about the auction. Matter of fact, people are excited to bid on goods and services provided by Electra's own." Warming up, Jarred kept talking. "People want to bid on the fire chief checking their homes for safety issues. For the grocer to provide free fruits and vegetables for a month. For Mrs. Walker to make them a couple of pies for Thanksgiving."

"Those are legitimate things people want. You, on the other hand, are auctioning off your bachelorhood."

Jarred looked stunned. "Hell, no, I'm not. I'm just auctioning off my time, that's all. The lady who bids on me will have me at her beck and call for a whole week."

Picking up another book, she checked the spine for damage, then set it in the shelving rack. "It sounds like you're signing up to be a gigolo, and I don't want any part of that."

"I'm not going gigolo-ing, and that's a fact." He had the nerve to look somewhat embarrassed. "Sheesh, Serena. The things you think about."

To her shame, her cheeks heated. "I'm not thinking about… about you gigolo-ing." Of course, now that he'd mentioned it, she could hardly think about anything else but the idea of too-handsome Jarred Riddell tucked neatly between a pair of white summer sheets.

Resolutely, she pulled herself back toward reality. She and Jarred had been pals for too long for her silly crush to get in the way.

"I don't need to advertise for sex, by the way."

"That's good to know," she said sarcastically. "'Cause I was getting nervous."

He looked her over, seeming to take in her long khaki skirt, black T-shirt and sensible leather sandals in one fell swoop.

She twitched a bit, wishing her hips were a little less generous. A little more lithe.

But instead of looking at her as though she was in need of a makeover, his gaze sparkled with humor. "Maybe you're just jealous 'cause no one's asked you for a service," he teased.

"I am not jealous. But, thanks for reminding me about that." She couldn't quite hold off the hurt in her voice. After all, she did know about the auction, and she had been feeling a little left out that no one had asked her to donate a single thing.

Of course, she probably shouldn't have taken the slight to heart. After all, what could she do, anyway? Offer to lend the populace books?

"That came out kind of harsh. I didn't mean anything in a bad way. Sorry."

She waved off his apology. Because, well, it wasn't really his fault that no one ever saw her as much more than the smart, superefficient woman who managed the library. She was simply Serena. Serena, whose daddy got gored by a bull.

Serena, who had gone to college on scholarship. Serena, the gal who took an inordinate amount of pride in list making and being prepared for any emergency.

She simply didn't have that good ol' boy personality, or the female equivalent, that Jarred did. No, her personality seemed to lean more toward the cool, distant, professional type.

But that was beside the point. "All I'm saying is that people should just want to give money to the community fund because it's the right thing to do. Not to get something out of it."

"That way of thinking is just another example of you living in some kind of fairy-tale dreamworld, Serena. People don't do things out of the goodness of their hearts. Not anymore they don't."

Had they ever?

Sticking to reason, Serena kept on talking as if Jarred hadn't uttered a word. She knew from experience that it was best to ignore most of the words coming out of his mouth instead of trying to figure out how his mind worked. "Second, even if you did get auctioned off—which I don't doubt you will—that doesn't mean that Veronica What's-Her-Name is going to be the one paying for your time. Chances are, she probably won't even go to the auction."

"Sure she will. Everyone's going. And, it's Snow. *Veronica Snow,*" he enunciated with exaggerated slowness. "And I don't need her to do a damn thing except bid on me. But first she needs to like me." His broad shoulders slumped. "Which, at the moment, she does not."

"Jarred, I'm not ever going to say yes to this crazy plan. Never."

He leaned closer, carrying with him the scent of his cologne. "Never's a long time, sweetheart."

Didn't she know that! "Don't 'sweetheart' me. Go ask

someone else for help." Like someone who he'd flirted with already. Someone else. Anyone else.

Down went the brim of his hat. Up went his chin. Somehow he managed to look at her under the shadow of that hat and not look completely ridiculous. "Well, see, it's not quite that easy."

"Why not?"

"Because no one else wants to take me seriously."

"They would if you ever were serious for more than an hour at a time."

"I'm serious when I'm at the ranch. I'm in charge of all the hands, you know."

"I know." Jarred's family had one of the biggest ranches in the county with at least a dozen horses and a hundred head of cattle. And oil rigs galore. "I know you work hard at home. But you also spent three years trying to be a rodeo star. And, well, we know how that ended up."

"We can't all be like Trent."

Immediately, she felt bad. Jarred's youngest brother, Trent, was a bona fide rodeo star, with endorsements and everything.

But, well, someone had to tell Jarred the truth.

She bit her lip. It might as well be her. "You also spend most of your time goofing around Electra. You sleep late and party too much. And this latest goal of yours is nothing if not laughable."

Serena noticed something flicker in his eyes—at least, as much of those eyes that she could see. "Listen, I am serious about Veronica. And you know the same as I do that rodeoing is a hard life. And I don't 'goof around Electra,' as you put it. I spend the majority of my days making our ranch run right. I only make it look easy."

"I suppose."

"And as a matter of fact, I am completely serious about

being taken seriously. I need some polish. I need some help. And there's no one at home who can help me. Gwen's got her hands full helping out with Virginia. She doesn't have time to worry about social graces, if you get my drift. And Gwen, well, Gwen is more the type of woman to have around when you need a gunfighter."

Jarred did have a point. Gwen was nearing sixty and was a nice lady. But she probably had never given much thought to Jarred's manners—or lack of them.

Actually, the Riddells' housekeeper was definitely more the go-to gal when your toilet needed scrubbing, your horse had colic or your transmission was leaking fluid.

Just to tease him, Serena said, "What? Gwen never taught you to take off your hat when you enter a room?"

As if she'd just quoted the Gospel, off went that hat so fast, Serena found herself blinking at his blond hair. She had forgotten it was cut so short. It had been a long time since she'd seen his head uncovered.

And that was a good indication of just how little she knew him these days, a shadow of how they used to get along.

When they were younger and in 4-H together, they'd talked quite a bit. Her awkwardness had seemed to amuse him to no end.

And, well, he'd been a year older in school. He'd been handsome and popular and fun. Oh, she'd done all right back then. And they had stayed good friends. But every so often she'd find herself looking his way a bit too long. Imagining him kissing her under the bleachers. Thinking about Jarred asking her to dance to something soft and slow.

But it had never happened.

Yep, back then, he'd showed his calf and she'd showed her collie at the fair. Before she knew it, they'd been buddies of a sort. Oh, nothing like best friends, but good ones. They'd hung out at ball games. They'd take a couple of turns around the dance floor whenever there was a dance. Then she'd gone off to college and the years had passed.

When she returned to Electra, they'd chat a bit whenever they could, but she was busy at her library, and Jarred was busy being Jarred.

Yet now, here he was, visiting her in the library and asking a favor.

Jarred looked pretty darn awkward without a hat on his head, and that was a fact. Almost naked, really. Maybe he should've kept it on?

Fidgeting with the brim again and again, he said, "So, Serena, you know my mama died years ago. Back when Cal, Trent and me were just boys."

"I know."

"And, you know how my dad's second wife kind of took off and left just weeks after Virginia was born."

What she remembered was that he'd been hit hard by the woman's departure. "I remember that, too. But I'm not quite sure what it has to do with your present situation."

"I'm getting to that. Soon after, my dad went a little crazy and then oil came and then things got really twisted and turned. I had my hands full just trying to make sure Virginia was looked after. The only thing Gwen did was clean." Something dark entered his eyes. "The only 'good' woman my dad's taken out took one look at us and our loud ways and scooted off like lightning."

Serena had heard rumors about that giant house with boys running roughshod over anyone who dared to enter. "I can't imagine why."

He held up a hand. "We were pretty…rambunctious, but our hearts were in the right place, and that's the truth."

"Is it?"

"Almost." Looking apologetic, he added, "We were kind of difficult. Some might say things are still like that. Now,

Ginny's getting a little wild, being home around cows and men all day. She's in dire need of feminine influence."

"And for that you need Veronica Snow?"

"I do, Seri. Truly."

"I don't know…"

"Think about it? I'll pay you for your time."

Serena figured it was no stretch to say Jarred Riddell was definitely not an easy man for her to be around. He was a handful—and she had no desire to be anywhere near his hands. "I appreciate your story. But, I think it's time you left. I'm not going to tutor you, or educate you, or whatever you want to call it. Besides, you're rich enough to hire a professional charm-school teacher. You ought to do that."

He blinked. "You want me to contact some snooty gal and ask for help? Not a chance."

"I think you should think on that again. A professional girl might be your only hope. A professional gal would know exactly what a woman like Veronica expects as far as manners and charms."

The look that flashed in his eyes was a bit surprising. Gone was the good ol' boy. In his place was a man who was used to getting what he wanted. "I wish you'd reconsider. I need to get Veronica to notice me. She's exactly what my family needs. I know she's what Virginia needs. She's already starting to cuss like a cowhand. Ginny needs a role model with class."

Serena knew it shouldn't bother her that Jarred never even thought about her in that way. But it did. "I've given you my answer, and it's final." Picking up a stack of DVDs from the return slot, she started scanning them into the library's database. Though a child could scan, Serena did her best to look as if it took a lot of concentration. "Now, I've got things to do here. You need to move on your way."

"Well, thanks for nothing, Serena." Just as he pivoted on

one heel, he jarred the portable mystery book rack. Twelve neatly stacked mysteries flew to the floor. "Crap!"

Every single person in their triple-wide trailer turned library looked up and glared. At her.

Of course. Things never were Jarred's fault. "Please leave. Now," she hissed under her breath. "You're disturbing everyone."

"I'm not giving up."

"You should." Pointing to the door, she said, "Off you go, now. I've got things to do."

"I'll be back," he said, rushing out the door, the metal bar giving a hearty slap-slap as it opened and shut with the motion.

Serena's assistant, Hannah, wandered over and waved a hand across her rouged cheeks. "Lord have mercy but that Jarred Riddell is something else. No man should be put together so well. It's almost sinful."

Serena wondered once again if she was the only one on earth who was immune to Jarred Riddell's charms. As that pesky image of him stark naked flew into her brain, she privately amended that thought.

She was *almost* immune. As she recalled just how aware of him she'd been, she corrected herself again.

She wasn't immune to his charms at all. Fact was, she was smitten.

Not that anyone would need to know that. "He's something else, all right."

Hannah's permed graying curls bounced a bit as she fussed with a stack of biographies that were on loan from one of the bigger branches in their library system. "I couldn't help but overhear. Are you going to help him with his predicament?"

"Help him catch a snooty society girl? I don't think so."

Still looking out the window at Jarred's retreating form,

watching him slide into the driver's seat of his yellow Corvette, Hannah sniffed. "That is a crying shame, don't you know. If I were younger, I'd do everything I could to latch on to him. My, but he is such a *fine*-looking man."

Yes, Jarred was, but that didn't mean she was going to turn her life—and her heart—upside down to make him happy. She had enough to worry about without taking on Jarred's bite-size problems.

The fact that he was gorgeous and available didn't mean a damn thing at all.

Chapter Two

"So I heard you got your butt handed to you by an extremely efficient librarian," Junior said when Jarred pulled up next to him in their oversize carport.

"I left Serena forty-five minutes ago. How'd you hear about that so fast?"

"Good news always travels like lightning."

"Good news and embarrassments." Looking around the area, things seemed suspiciously quiet. "What's going on around here?"

"Trent got in a few hours ago."

"That's good." With all the emotional upheaval of trying to get his manners fixed up, he'd forgotten Trent had a sizable break in between shows. "Where is he?"

"Out in the barn, checking up on his horse. And I'm wondering how to get another year out of this pickup."

Though they could've bought ten new Chevys, buying a new truck when the old one wasn't dead wasn't Junior's way. But as Jarred looked at the rusted fender he thought maybe even Junior would agree that it was time for a trade-in. "That may be a lost cause."

"Maybe." With a look of irritation at the old truck, his brother stepped away from the old Chevy. "I've got to meet with the accountants this afternoon and Gwen's got something going on with one of her grandkids. Do you mind looking after Virginia?"

For the first time all day, Jarred felt genuinely happy. "Not at all. Where is she?"

"In the house."

"I'm on my way." Stepping into the house, he waved a greeting to Gwen, who was watering an assortment of plants she kept in fancy pots in the breakfast area. "Hey. Where's Ginny?"

The water pitcher paused. "She came home from a playdate and fell asleep after her snack," she said with a smile. "They went on a walking field trip today. I'm starting to think she probably did more hop, skip and jumping than walking. She's plumb wore out. Why?"

"Cal's got things to do, so I'm on Ginny duty."

"Are you sure you have time?"

"'Course I do. You've got plans, right?"

"I do. Little JennieLynn's showing her pony this weekend for the first time, so we're having a trial run at the barn."

Gwen's people had shown their horses in shows for generations. "Hope she does real good."

"Thank you. Now you have a good time with our girl, but I better warn you, she wants to play zoo when she wakes up. She was gathering all her animals together when she fell asleep."

A wave of tenderness washed over him. "After what I've been through today, I'll be happy to play zoo as long as she wants. Get on, now."

"All right. Um, I made a chicken-and-rice casserole."

Jarred gently kissed her on the cheek. "I know we'll all appreciate that. Thank you."

"It probably won't be as good as one of yours, but it will do."

"It will, in a heartbeat." Jarred was no stranger to fussing around in the kitchen. When their mother had died, it seemed all of them had taken on as much as they could. His dad was a good man, but their mother's death had hit him hard. He spent as much time as he could traveling or in seclusion in his office.

His emotional departure meant that the rest of them had to pick up the slack. So, they'd each done their part. Junior was organized and book smart. Most folks said he was the one who'd inherited all the brains from their mother's branch of the family. He was also a man of few words.

Jarred, in addition to seeing to the day-to-day needs of the ranch, had become their domestic goddess. He didn't want to let it be known, but he certainly knew his way around a laundry room and could throw together more meals than anyone imagined.

Trent was the most like the rest of the men in the Riddell family. He could nurse horses, fix engines and understood the land as well as the back side of his hand. He was also near famous. He'd found a lot of success on the rodeo circuit, and had garnered more sponsors, buckles and women than Jarred could imagine.

It was hard to believe. And hard to believe that the three of them were as successful as they were.

'Course, they'd had their challenges. Their stepmother, Carolyn, had been lovely in the beginning, and had given their daddy a girl. Luckily for the boys, they'd been too busy following their own pursuits to get too attached to the snake. Only their father had become bitter when she'd left.

But their feelings for Carolyn's daughter were a whole other story. From the moment he'd held Ginny in his arms, a fierce protectiveness had run through Jarred that was more powerful than anything he'd ever felt before.

He knew he wasn't alone in feeling that way. His brothers, too, were wrapped around her tiny fingers.

Yep. He might never give his heart to a woman like his father had, but he had his little sister. Ginny, at least, was always easy to love.

He used the hour she was sleeping to sort through the mail, return a few phone calls and read part of the paper. Then, just as he was getting ready to wake her from her nap, he heard her distinctive high-pitched voice.

Without delay, he hightailed it to Ginny's room. Her eyes widened when she saw him. Then she smiled. "Hi."

"Hey, sugar." Gamely, he sat down on the floor next to her, spreading his feet out in front of him. "I heard you went on a big field trip today."

"I did. We saw all kinds of things. Electra's clock tower and the ice-cream shop and the library and the auction block."

He laughed. "That would be the parcel of land where the mayor wants to put the new community center."

"Well, there's a big stand there, so Mrs. Weaver called it the auction block."

"Were you a good girl today?"

Quickly, she looked away. Picking up a toy tiger, she exclaimed, "Terry the tiger escaped from the zoo!"

"Virginia Riddell, did you get in a fight?"

"Almost."

"Virginia Ann?"

"Yes, sir, but it wasn't my fault. Billy said I ran like a girl."

"You are a girl."

"I know. But I don't want to run like one. Anyways, Billy stopped teasing me after I hit him."

Jarred sighed. "And then what happened?"

"Billy told on me. He's such a sissy." She picked up another toy tiger. "This is Jamal."

Jarred picked up Jamal. "Billy's not a sissy for telling on you."

"Sure he is. You and Trent and Cal never go tell Daddy if one of you hits the other."

He winced. He and his brothers did have an awful habit of hitting first and talking later. "We shouldn't be fighting. Neither should you."

"Can we just play tigers now? Jamal knows a secret spot by Princess Virginia's bed. Come on!"

He was tempted to chew on her, but he knew it would do no good. What she needed was feminine instruction. And he was working on that.

Together, they crawled on the carpet, moving their tigers along make-believe deserts and jungles.

Virginia giggled and he smiled.

And an hour later, when she crawled up into his lap for a cartoon break, he leaned his head back against the couch and counted his blessings. This little girl was a piece of work, and that was a fact.

Too bad all women weren't as easily pleased.

A bit of uneasiness floated through him as he imagined what life with Veronica Snow would be like. He imagined only the best would make her happy.

He had gobs of money, so that was no problem. Heck, he'd gladly buy her diamonds for all her fingers if that meant she'd show Ginny a thing or two.

He'd learn to speak a little bit better and learn about table manners if she'd consider going out to eat with him.

He'd try his best to watch his cussing and wash the dirt off his clothes five times a day if she'd ever consent to tilt that perfect face up to his and agree to let him kiss her.

Surely those lips would be as sweet as they looked from afar. They had to be.

And then, well, then he'd have it made. He'd have a beautiful woman in his life and Ginny would stop trying to cuss her way out of kindergarten.

Serena Higgins was just going to have to come around to his way of thinking and help him win over Veronica. Soon.

Chapter Three

"There she is," Hannah said with awe in her voice, as if she was announcing Miss America. "That there is Veronica Snow herself crossing this very parking lot in a fuchsia silk skirt and extremely sexy high heels." After pausing a moment to admire the woman's fashion sense, Hannah whistled low. "Isn't she something?"

"She is, at that," Serena agreed. From their pair of chairs in front of the Electric Dip—the town's somewhat hippie-inspired ice-cream shop—Serena licked her chocolate cone and wondered what Veronica did all day that warranted so many fancy clothes.

Why, the last Serena had heard, the Dallas socialite spent most of her time on the internet and on her cell phone, chatting with all the people who'd never heard of Electra. Serena figured Veronica could have saved herself a whopping dry-cleaning bill for that.

Serena had always felt more comfortable in her usual attire of jeans, cotton blouses and occasional broomstick skirts. She owned two pairs of boots and they got her through just about anything.

Her feet probably wouldn't know what to do in four-inch heels.

Hannah was eyeing those high-heeled pumps as if she wanted to rush out to Neiman Marcus and get a pair.

"Serena, how much do you think shoes like that cost? Eighty dollars?"

Serena wasn't sure, but she could have sworn she'd read something in *People* magazine about prices of shoes. Each pair highlighted had been at least three digits. "More, I'm thinking."

As Veronica gracefully walked alone on the sidewalk, her expression a cool mask, Serena started to feel a bit guilty. After all, Veronica Snow was new in town and beautiful and rich, but she had problems, too. "How's her mother doing? Have you heard?"

In a split second, all traces of shoe envy vanished from Hannah's face. "Last I heard, her mama wasn't doing too well at all," she said with a frown. "Her blood pressure is spiking something awful. I guess that blood disease she has ain't doing her no favors."

"That's a shame."

"Uh-huh. Pete Ross over at the bank told me that Veronica was trying to find someone to come in part-time and help with that big old house. Seems Midge gets all weepy and nervous every time Veronica mentions the idea of selling that big old place."

"It's got to be tough, caring for a mother who's ailing like she is."

"You said it, Serena. Well, at least they discovered what was wrong. Used to be, I thought what she needed was more to do. But rumor has it that she won't be around for too much longer."

Serena was just about to suggest that they pay a visit to Midge, or offer to help in some way when a slight breeze flicked Veronica's skirt a bit. The hem fluttered a few inches north, revealing a perfect pair of long lean legs.

Serena bit into her cone and tried to recall if she'd ever had slim legs like that. Maybe in sixth grade?

Hannah gasped. "Ooh, I think she's coming this way."

And sure enough, there she was. Taking refuge in chocolate, Serena swiped an errant drip with her tongue. She'd just crunched on the rim of her cone when Veronica stepped right up to the walk-up window that Paula McCall, owner of the Electric Dip, had installed last summer.

"Do you have anything low-fat today?" Veronica asked, her voice all soft and low and kind of musical.

Paula shook her head sadly. "I told Gavin about your low-fat idea, but he's not sold on it yet. The lowest-cal item we have at the moment is still just sherbet, Miss Snow. But it is raspberry and we made it fresh this morning. Want a scoop?"

"I suppose. I'll take it in a cup instead of a cone, though."

When she held a cup loaded high with raspberry sherbet, Veronica turned their way. Every chair in the little stone patio was taken.

Serena waited for Veronica to take the hint and move along.

But then Hannah—being Hannah—waved a hand. "Veronica! Veronica Snow! Would you care to join Serena and me?"

"Oh, thank you," Veronica said, looking relieved as she took a seat. "I really didn't want to eat this standing up. I'd have dripped on my new blouse for sure." Before Serena could take a furtive glance at her own top, Veronica turned her way. "I'm sure we've met but I'm afraid I can't remember your name."

"This here is Serena Higgens," Hannah interjected quickly. "Serena and I are librarians. Well, actually, Serena is the *real* librarian. She went to college and got her degree on scholarship. I'm just her assistant."

Veronica held out her hand. "It's a pleasure to meet you. I'm Veronica Snow. I just moved here from Dallas. Maybe you know my mom, Midge? She grew up here, then moved back a few years ago."

Hannah smiled. "I know your mother well. She used to visit the library quite a bit. Oh, how she loved those cat mysteries!"

"She always was a reader." Looking glum, Veronica spooned some sherbet into her mouth.

Hannah smiled gently. "So, how is she doing?"

"All right, thanks for asking." Her perfect features cracked. "Actually, my mother's not doing very well at all. Little by little, she's slowly fading from me. Some days it's real hard to try and find the woman who raised me inside the shell that seems to have surrounded her. But she does seem to be happier now that I'm here. At least, that's what the doctor says."

"You moved out here for her, right?" Hannah asked.

"Right. I hope you don't mind me saying so, but this place isn't really my style."

"I imagine it's not." When Veronica looked at her in surprise, Serena attempted to explain herself. "I mean, I heard you used to model in Dallas."

Hannah leaned forward. "Is that true?"

"I did. Well, I modeled for Neiman's and a few other department stores. I made a lot of friends that way. Then, when I got a little old, I started working with some of the women's groups."

"I imagine the shopping here is a far cry from what you're used to."

"You would imagine correctly," Veronica said around another spoonful of sherbet. "But it's all right. I don't need much, and, well, Hebron is less than an hour away and has a lot of cute shops and a very good hair salon. I figure if I can just get over there one or two days a week, get to Dallas for another few days once a month, why, I'll be able to survive living here for a while…."

Unspoken was that Veronica was obviously only going to stay until her mother passed on.

Something about it all made Serena uncomfortable, though she knew that was the exact opposite way she should be feeling. What Veronica was doing was commendable. Here she was, giving up pretty much her whole life to see to her mother's comfort.

But, unfortunately, Serena was also very aware of Jarred's feelings. He was crushing on the girl in the worst way, dreaming about a future with her, but he truly had no idea that the town he loved could never stay his home if he hooked up with the beauty.

"Survive?"

"Sorry. I guess I sound like I'm putting this place down. I don't mean to. This little town is real nice. It's just not me, you know?"

Looking at Veronica's diamond earrings and perfect posture, Serena nodded. "Oh, I know."

Hannah gently kicked her before turning back to Veronica, a model of sweetness. "Things are slow here."

After carefully spooning another minute portion of sherbet into her mouth, Veronica said, "They sure are."

Around them, the stand got more crowded. Serena tried to assume that it was crowded only because the temperature was reaching a hundred, but she suspected it had more to do with Veronica's presence. Gossip had been slow lately and everyone was anxious to hear something new.

Serena was just trying to figure out something pleasant to ask when Veronica's face fell.

"Oh, no," she murmured.

"What's wrong?" Serena asked.

"It's that cowboy. Everywhere I go, he seems to be there, too." A wary expression appeared on her perfect porcelain face. "It's uncanny. I'd call him a stalker except our meetings seem too coincidental for that. And, well, he does seem fairly harmless. But here he is, coming this way again."

A sense of dark foreboding glided over Serena. Slowly, she glanced down the sidewalk. There, sure enough, came Jarred. From the way he was walking, it looked as if he was on a heck of a mission, too. A mission to join them.

"That's Jarred," Hannah said helpfully. "Jarred Riddell. He used to be a rodeo cowboy. His youngest brother still is."

"But now?"

"Now, he's just plain rich."

A tiny spark of interest flared in Veronica's eyes before she looked away from him in distaste. "I would've never guessed. He seems to wear the same clothes every day. The way he stares at me makes me nervous. Like I'm his favorite lasagna or something."

"He does seem intent on you," Hannah agreed. "It's disconcerting!"

"Hey, y'all," Jarred said the moment he approached with a toothy smile. "Enjoying the day?"

"As much as we can in this heat!" Hannah replied, all smiles.

"It's a hot one for sure," Jarred agreed. "'Course, it is July in Texas." Jarred rocked back on his heels a bit.

That's when Serena noticed he was holding a bottle in his hand. A bottle of…tobacco juice? As the liquid swished around inside of it, Veronica stiffened.

Serena couldn't blame her for that. It was a nasty habit. As inconspicuously as possible, she pointed to his cheek and shook her head.

He rolled his eyes, then went to the garbage can and threw out the rest of his chew. Veronica eyed him warily when he returned. "Sorry about that," he said. "I practically forgot I had a cheek full of chew."

Oh, he was so hopeless! Serena fought off a grin.

Luckily, Hannah had raised four boys, had seven grand-children and never got fazed by much. Giving Jarred a little wink and a smile, she said, "So, handsome, what are you up to today?"

"Other than being six foot two? Nothing much," he said with a smile as he sauntered a little closer.

Serena groaned at the bad joke. Veronica, on the other hand, seemed to be trying to figure out what in the heck he was talking about.

As oblivious as ever, Jarred yanked over an empty chair from another table and sat. "I've been doing a little work out in the barns."

"Barns?"

"We've got a couple. Some of the farthest ones were run-ning a little low on supplies." Veronica couldn't seem to be able to look away from the tragedy in front of her. Her sherbet melted in the dish in front of her, completely forgotten. "What about you ladies?"

"About what you see," Hannah replied, pointing to her very short sugar cone. "Eating ice cream and trying to stay cool."

He smiled. "Y'all look so pretty, it must be working. I don't see a drop of sweat on any of you."

Serena groaned.

After a glance her way, Jarred backpedaled. "Oh, I'm sorry, I guess I should have said, 'perspiration,' huh?"

Serena winced. Surely Jarred didn't think she was going to pull out her manners book and give him tips right that minute? Wordlessly, she shook her head in a subtle warning to *stop*.

"What?"

Oh, of course he wouldn't know what she meant. He was so…clueless! Why didn't he even know enough to realize that no woman wanted to see what he was doing? Ever?

"You want to go get yourself some ice cream and join us,

Jarred?" Hannah asked. "Veronica was just telling us about her mama."

"I'll skip the ice cream but stay and enjoy your company, if you don't mind." As if he was on a talk show, he sprawled out into their space, kicking his feet out in front of them. Feet that were covered in work boots. And work boots that smelled as if they'd been tromping in fields with cattle and horses.

For a moment, Serena looked fondly at him. Jarred wasn't a man to hire someone to do tough work. No, he did work hard. His hands were calloused and rough, and those boots of his illustrated just how much he did.

She was used to such a sight. So was Hannah.

But Veronica, well, Veronica obviously wasn't. Her nose wrinkled. "You know, I had best be on my way," she said as she picked up her purse.

"So soon?" Jarred pointed to her dish. "But your ice cream ain't half gone."

"I know. I, um, have suddenly lost my appetite."

The moment Veronica stood up, so did he. In his haste, Jarred knocked his chair over. Which made him grab for it.

Which made Serena's chocolate ice-cream cone slip from her hands and fall...right onto her lap. It took less than a second to feel the sticky melted ice cream seep through the material.

"Jarred, look what you did!" In disgust, she jumped to her feet just as Veronica quickened her pace and strode out to the parking lot. Holding the skirt away from her skin, Serena eyed the runny brown mess oozing down her front. "This is disgusting."

He frowned. "Crap. I'm really sorry about that, sugar. I don't know what happened. My hand must have slipped."

"Now I've got to go change."

"Luckily all your things are wash-and-wear," Hannah said.

"You'll be able to toss that skirt in the washer after a good soak, no problem."

Just as Serena was about to smile her way, Hannah's brow furrowed. "No, that skirt is not like Veronica's lovely outfit at all. If that had gotten soiled, well, it certainly would have been a tragedy."

"Perhaps," Serena said drily.

Picking up her purse, Hannah tossed two napkins in the trash before snatching her keys. "I'll go on back to work, Serena. You take your time getting cleaned up."

"I'll be there as soon as I can."

When they were relatively alone again Jarred stepped a bit closer. "Why do you think Veronica ran off like that? It sure seemed sudden."

"You don't know? It was because you've got cow dung on your boot."

Experimentally, he lifted a boot and sniffed hard. "I can't help that. It's what cows do. I told y'all I was out working in the west pasture."

"Well, she thinks you smell."

"I don't. I mean, not anything other than my usual scent. And I did shower and shave this morning."

For an instant, Serena let herself lean closer, and definitely did catch a scent that was one-hundred-percent Jarred. Underneath the manure and dust and tobacco was soap and mint and expensive aftershave.

How was it that she never had been able to completely block out his attributes?

And how was it that he never seemed to notice hers?

Feeling peevish, she said, "Next time you're around her, get rid of that bottle of spit. And for that matter, don't carry it around me, either."

He had the gall to grin. "I can't promise you that. But I will promise that I'll do my best not to dump ice cream on you again." Leaning close, he brushed two fingers along her cheek.

"What did you do that for?"

"You've got chocolate everywhere, honey." Smiling, he kissed her on the cheek. "You taste good, though."

A little tremor coursed through her. She bit her lip, hoping he wouldn't notice. "Conversations like this are why Veronica is never going to think you're a gentleman, Jarred."

He slumped. "No, conversations like this prove I need your help. As soon as possible."

"Well, it sure can't be today. I've got to go home and switch skirts."

"But soon?"

"Maybe." She never had been able to refuse him much. "I'll let you know."

Tipping his hat, he grinned. "That's why I love you, Serena."

As she watched him walk away, Serena reminded herself that he didn't really love her.

And that he would never be a very good boyfriend anyway. He'd been too hurt by his mom's death and his stepmother's taking off to trust much.

But sometimes, when he smiled at her and said those things…and kissed her cheek…she kind of wished he did.

Chapter Four

Jarred dreaded the family financial meetings with Victor Owens more than a root canal. On the third Tuesday of each month the banker stopped by and talked shop with Cal Sr. and his three sons. Their father, being the way he was, always liked Jarred, Jnior and Trent to sit there, too, seeing how their inheritance went three ways.

Jarred understood the reasoning. On paper, the whole little get-together sounded like a real fine idea. But in actuality, he considered it a waste of time. Not a one of them were going to ever learn to work together all that well.

And never had the three boys and their dad been in a meeting in which they didn't fuss and fight. It wasn't anything personal. It was just the way it was.

Since the moment Calvin Riddell had found oil in the middle of nowhere, Jarred and his brothers had been managing things pretty well. As the years progressed, they'd come to a pretty good division of power, too. Junior basically handled all the financial aspects of things. He monitored the investments, studied the portfolios and researched ways to diversify the Riddell brand. Jarred, being that he was the oldest son and not near as good with figures as Junior, had taken over the day-to-day operations of the ranch. Trent, well, they let Trent travel the rodeo circuit and be a superstar.

But every month, Victor Owens thought it would be a good

idea for all five of them to discuss things all in one room, which was kind of akin to putting a barrel of monkeys in a cage at the zoo. Chaos always ensued.

Fact was, their cozy little group of five got on Jarred's nerves something awful. Their dad never had had a way with numbers. Actually, numbers flew by his daddy faster than dust in an October storm. Jarred would be forced to sit and listen as Victor went over things two and three times, taking into account his daddy's terrible business sense and Trent's inability to grow up.

As Victor repeated something for the seventh time, Jarred felt his attention drift. What he really wanted to do was get started with Serena's lessons. If she'd ever give him the go-ahead.

Fact was, he needed her help. Needed it in a bad way, and that was no exaggeration, either. Veronica had looked at him as if he was the crap stuck on his boot when he'd joined those three women at the ice-cream shop. And that said a lot.

The problem was, he thought he'd been doing just fine. No, better than fine. How was he supposed to know that city girls didn't like their men chewing tobacco? Didn't city girls understand a man's need for Skoal?

Victor tapped the table with the end of his pencil. "Jarred, you with us, son?"

"Yes, sir." After a quick glance to his right, Jarred hastily flipped two pages in the notebook the financial advisor was walking them through—slow as molasses.

Next to him, Trent snickered.

Victor glanced his way over his half-moon glasses. "Any questions, gentlemen? I know we went through all of this last month, but I'd be happy to answer anything you'd be needing to know…"

Junior answered for all of them. "No, sir. We have no questions."

"All right, then. Well, I'll just continue explaining this account's forecast and then be on my way."

And so the meeting continued for another hour before thankfully—thankfully—Gwen rapped on the door before sticking her head in. Seconds later, Virginia peeked out around her legs.

Their father grinned. "Hey, peanut. You need something?"

Ginny nodded. "Uh-huh."

Gwen laughed. "I'm sorry to bother you, Mr. Riddell. It's just that I've promised the ladies' club that I'd help out at their meeting this afternoon. I'm going to be late unless I leave soon."

Jarred jumped to his feet. "I'd forgotten all about that. I'll take Ginny."

His father smiled at the little girl for a moment before glancing Jarred's way. "You don't mind, son?"

"Never." Quicker than a jackrabbit on a greyhound track, he hopped over and took Virginia's hand. "I'll talk to Junior about everything later," he promised, thanking his lucky stars for an excuse to leave the meeting.

He chuckled when he heard Trent moan as the heavy door closed behind them.

When they were in the hall and Virginia was all smiles again, Gwen crossed her arms in front of her chest. "You sure you're okay? I wouldn't have said I could help the garden club except your dad thought your meeting was going to end an hour ago."

Recalling everyone's fussing about the wording on one of the documents, Jarred said drily, "It should have. And believe me, I'm glad you knocked on the door. I was ready for a break anyway." Heck, he'd been ready to get out of there from the moment Victor had instructed them to open their financial folders.

"Those meetings do run long."

"They do." Thinking again about Serena and Veronica, he stepped a little closer to Gwen while Ginny wandered down the hall to see Scruffy, her cat. "Hey, um…Gwen, you're a girl."

One eyebrow arched. "I was at one time. I think when you hit your fifties you prefer to be classified as a 'woman,' though."

"All right. Woman. Um, as a woman, what do you think about me?"

"What?" Wariness filled her gaze.

"What do you think of me as a man," he sputtered. When she frowned, he attempted to clarify. "I mean, as a girl." Thinking he might need to be more politically correct, he hastened to change his words. "I mean, as a woman. I mean, as a girl-woman who didn't live here like an aunt or something."

"I'm not really sure," she said slowly. "All that really comes to mind is that you don't pick up the clothes off your floor. What is it you want to know?"

He stopped pussyfooting around. "Here's the thing. I've been fixated on Veronica Snow something awful and have been doing everything I can to earn her interest, but not a thing has been working. Yesterday, I saw her sitting with Serena and Hannah at the ice-cream shop. But the moment I sat down, she got on out of there like her ass was on fire."

"What did Serena say about that?"

"Nothing of import. I need another opinion. Why do you think Veronica won't give me the time of day?"

"I don't know her real well, she's only been to two of the Electra Ladies Club meetings, but it might be because she's used to a different kind of guy." She paused meaningfully. "You know…a city guy."

"A guy who sits around in an office?"

"Maybe."

"I'm not that."

She practically hooted as she patted his shoulder. "You sure ain't. I think that would be a problem for her. Maybe for you, too. I mean, you can't be something you're not, right?"

"I can be different. I know I can. I just need some help learning how to be a little less rough around the edges. Want to help?"

"I wouldn't know the first thing how to do that. You should ask Serena to help. Y'all are good friends. Shoot, she knows you just about better than anyone. I'm sure she'll give you a try."

He slumped. Conveniently forgetting that he'd very recently vowed to have nothing to do with her, he said, "She might. If she has time."

"Serena's pretty busy. Maybe there's someone else?"

"I don't think so. Next to Veronica Snow, Serena's the most fancy girl in our town."

Looking him over, her face softened. "Look, if snagging Veronica is what you really want to do, I'd go try asking Serena again. She's got a good heart. And she's even been to New York City before. Serena knows a lot about *impressing* people."

Jarred knew Gwen was right about that. Fact was, Serena was a pretty thing, and had the kind of figure most men would only dream about. And she had a beautiful smile, too. "You may have a point." Feeling completely stressed, he pulled out his package of chew and positioned a wad in his cheek.

Watching him and his nicotine fit, she frowned. "Are you sure you can't just forget about Veronica?"

"I don't think so. We need a gal like that around here."

Ginny picked that very moment to squeal. "Oh, crap! Jarred, come here, wouldja? I got bit! Shit!"

Gwen and Jarred both flinched.

Gwen looked at him long and good before she turned

toward the back door. "The thing of it is, Jarred, you may think you want Veronica here…but it might not be the place for her." As Ginny let out another torrent of swearwords, Gwen sighed. "Don't forget to wash out her mouth, now."

As Gwen ran out the door, Jarred marched to the kitchen. "Virginia Ann, where the heck did you learn to swear like that?"

"I don't know." She looked at her feet and held up a finger. Blood ran down one side of it. "But my finger really does hurt." Kneeling down, Jarred kissed the top of her head as he hoisted her onto his hip. "Let's go get you cleaned up. And then you're going to listen to me and stop cussing, 'kay?"

"'Kay. Then can we go see if the horses want some apples?"

"Maybe," he murmured. Because he could hardly ever tell her no, he added, "And maybe we'll go riding, too."

"Thank you, Jarred."

"Anytime, sweetheart. Anytime."

IT WAS A HORRIBLE MAIL DAY. Serena's college loan, rent and car bills had all talked and decided to make their way to her home in one neat little trip. All three bills had been lying on her entryway floor when she'd opened up her apartment that evening. There was hardly even any junk mail to soften the blow.

Picking up the letters, Serena grimaced. You'd think the post office would have the grace to try and space them out every once in a while.

Slumping against the back of her father's old easy chair, Serena nibbled her lip. How was she going to manage things?

She was still trying to figure out how to pay everything and still eat when her sister, Tracy, knocked. Once a week, Tracy went to an exercise class at the Y, then came over to Serena's for a glass of wine and catch-up.

Usually Tracy was too nice to point out the obvious differences in their lifestyles. She was married and spent her days home with a four-year-old little boy. She and her husband definitely didn't have the *Lifestyles of the Rich and Famous* way of life, but it sure was a whole lot fuller than Serena's.

After guiding her to the kitchen and pouring them both a glass of wine, the two of them sat down to chat. Tracy's news centered around Jesse, her boy.

Serena focused solely on the bills she needed to pay.

Sipping from her glass of Chardonnay, Tracy listened intently to Serena's laundry list of troubles. "Since you've already refused my offer of a loan, I'm a little at a loss of what you should do."

"I think I need a part-time job, just for a little while."

"How are you going to do that? You already work forty hours a week at the library." Before Serena could reply, Tracy continued. "I know you do like that job, but they pay you next to nothing! Maybe you should quit and find something else to do."

The thought of quitting the library was like having all her teeth pulled and dentures put in. It was just unthinkable. "But I love my job. I worked really hard to get it, too."

"It's good you love it, because you sure aren't working for the pay."

"It's easy for you to say. Bubba makes a good living selling insurance."

"He does, and that's a fact. Plus, I decided to get married instead of get a fancy master's in library science. I'm not spending my days dreading mail delivery. Those bills of yours are making you miserable. You know I'm right."

"I know." Only her sister could make Serena's goals of getting a higher education into a bad thing. But Serena knew

Tracy wasn't trying to be mean. "I know you're trying to help, but quitting isn't an option. And before you even suggest it again, no, I don't want a loan. And, I'm not going to ask Mom for help, either."

Tracy frowned. "Money's been really tight since Daddy got laid off in the fall." Then she almost smiled. "Hey, there's always Pete Ross over at the bank."

"What are you talking about?"

"You know. He's had a crush on you for ages. I bet he'd help you get a loan." She waggled her eyebrows up and down in a Groucho Marx way. "I bet he'd give you a personal loan if you agreed to go out with him."

Pete Ross. Wasn't that how it always was? Pete was a perfectly good man, who was decent-looking and had a perfectly good job. And he liked her. But was she interested in him?

Not even a little bit. "I can't do that. It wouldn't be right."

"You've got to do something."

"Not start dating men in order to use them."

Tracy drummed her fingers on the table. "All right. Maybe… maybe…I know! You could start giving blood? I read somewhere that the money's pretty good."

"Ha, ha." She'd have to give away every drop in her veins to make a difference. "No thanks. You know how I am with needles." Figuring she better dive in and tell her sister the whole truth, she said, "Um, actually, I do have an opportunity to make some extra cash, I've just been kind of slow to start up on it."

"What's that?"

Now that she'd brought up the subject, Serena wasn't sure how to go about sharing the whole unvarnished truth. "The other day, Jarred Riddell came to see me at the library."

Pressing one palm on her chest, Tracy struck a pose that would set the sweetest southern belle to shame. "He is so fine."

Privately, Serena agreed. He was fine. But that only served to remind her about just how different she and Jarred were. "Do you want to hear about this or not?"

"Of course I do. What did he want?"

"He offered me a job."

"To do what?"

She took a deep breath. "To give him charm-school lessons."

Tracy's mouth dropped open like a bass caught on the line. "Why on earth does he think he needs charm lessons? And why from you?"

"Because we're friends."

"I know you are. Y'all have been good buddies for ages." Her voice drifted off. Obviously she had a whole lot more in her mind than she was saying.

Against her will, Serena felt more than a bit, oh…put out. "Jarred wants to impress Veronica Snow. He's got this idea that if he's perfect, she'll bid on him at the Electra community auction next month." She took a deep breath and continued. "From then on, he imagines the two of them falling in love."

"Wow."

It was a mouthful! "Anyway, he thinks I have enough manners to help him, uh…achieve his goal."

"Oh…kay." Tracy looked her over. "Well, I never really thought of you as Electra's own Miss Manners, but I guess he does have a point. You do know how to eat and talk right. And, being a librarian and all, you could research all the finer points of etiquette."

"Thank you."

"And you are looking for a part-time job. How come you've been waiting to start?"

"No reason in particular," she fibbed. No way was she

going to let her sister know that just thinking about Jarred and Veronica together made her stomach knot.

"I still don't get it. You need some extra money, plus he's always been a good friend of yours. And, well, there are his biceps to think about. Those, alone, would be worth hours of my time."

He did have great arms. And abs, too. Forcing herself to only concentrate on her friend Jarred, she grappled with more excuses. "Jarred's a good guy, but, Trace, he never has taken directions well. He's so full of himself. And, I'm kind of worried that the manners thing would be a lost cause anyway. The last time I saw him, he was chewing tobacco right in front of Veronica. She got scared and ran off."

"That's easy enough to fix. And shoot, you wouldn't have to do all that much, I'm thinking. If you even get him halfway to being a gentleman, things will be a whole lot better." Picking up a bill, Tracy stared at Serena the way only an older sister could. "How much was he going to pay you?"

"I never thought to ask. I kind of felt uncomfortable even thinking about helping him for money."

"I hate to tell you this. But, if you won't accept a loan from me, you might not have a choice. You'd best get on the phone and see if you can stop by his place. Pronto."

"I don't want to go over to the Riddell ranch." She'd be on his home turf, plus there was enough testosterone around there to set her teeth on edge.

"You better. Otherwise he's going to find someone else or decide Veronica's not for him. Then you'll really be up a creek without a paddle." Waving a hand, she said, "The minute I leave, I want you to go get on the phone and become his etiquette advisor."

"I will. I guess you're right."

Tracy spoiled the moment by nodding. "Oh, I know I am. Call me later and tell me what happened."

The minute Tracy walked out her door, Serena picked up the phone and dialed Jarred's number. After speaking to Junior for a sec, he put Jarred on the line.

"Is this really Serena Higgens? Last I heard she was too busy to give me the time of day."

Oh, humble pie was so hard to eat! "It is. I was just wondering if you still needed some help with those charm-school lessons."

"You mean since yesterday?"

Serena supposed she deserved his sarcasm. "I…I thought maybe you might have changed your mind?"

"Why are you asking?"

"I've decided I have time to help you."

"Have you, now?"

Remembering Tracy's advice and staring at her bills, Serena told herself to be strong and move forward. "Is there any way I could come out and see you this evening?" she sputtered, sure her skin was turning so red and heated that someone would think she was sick. "We could talk about things."

"Sure." After a pause, he said, "Do you mind coming over?"

"No." She hadn't been to their ranch in years. "I could stop by in, say, an hour?"

"I'll be waiting, sugar. With bells on."

She gritted her teeth. "Good."

When she hung up, Serena tossed those bills against the wall and swore loudly. Making extra money shouldn't be so hard.

And neither should being around Jarred Riddell. All she needed to do was think that she was doing a favor for a friend. That was all. She was good at doing favors.

Chapter Five

"Who's coming over?" Trent asked from his position on the couch. Lately, he'd taken to sprawling on it at every opportunity, boots and all.

As if he was a patient in a counseling session or something.

Jarred scowled. "Serena Higgens is coming over, that's who. Get your feet off the couch."

One Roper lifted an inch before settling back on the supple leather with a puff of dust and grime. "Why?"

"Because you're going to mark up the leather, that's why." Jarred stared at him with disdain. "You're going to scratch that couch up something awful and ruin it." Sheesh, even he knew that much.

As slow as molasses, Trent plopped one foot after the other on the floor. "I don't know why you care so much about the state of leather around here all of a sudden. We bought this couch because it was supposed to be tough. That salesgirl said it could stand up to just about anything. Even us."

"She said it was tough, not indestructible."

"Why are you so touchy? And why have you invited Serena over here? Have y'all finally decided to go from friends to friends with benefits?"

"Hell, no." Wondering why Trent would even think such a

thing, he added, "There's nothing between us. Besides, she's a librarian."

"So? She's the sexiest librarian I ever saw. And I know there's something between y'all. There always has been."

Serena…sexy? "We're just friends, Trent. That's all."

"Have you ever kissed her?"

"No."

"That's too bad. That olive skin and green-hazel eyes of hers would just about drive me mad. And the way she fills out a pair of jeans…it's downright sinful."

The conversation was making Jarred slightly uncomfortable.

Because, well, now that he thought about it, his brother kind of had a point. Serena could fill out a pair of Lee jeans like no other.

But she was just his buddy…and he had a more refined type of girl in mind.

"So if you don't want to date her, why do you want her over here?"

"I offered her a job."

"Job?" Junior asked as he entered the room.

Snickering, Trent quipped, "Is Serena going to teach you to read?"

This questioning from his brothers was making him edgy. He didn't like feeling weak, especially not in front of them. Sarcastically, he said, "Maybe one day y'all will be smart enough to try out some original lines. Who knows? Maybe then your social life would improve."

As serious as ever, Junior looked him up and down. "Serena Higgens is a nice gal. What are you hiring her for?"

"I'm hiring her to help me get fancy."

Trent burst out laughing. Even Junior broke his usual solemn expression and smirked.

As Jarred watched them, his stomach churned. Shoot.

More than ever, his brothers were annoying him something awful.

Actually everything seemed to do that at the moment. More than ever, he felt like a contestant on *Wheel of Fortune*—and a bad one at that. Yes, the wheel in his life was continually spinning around in circles. He was living in fear that the darn wheel was fixin' to going to settle on *bankrupt* or *lose a turn* or whatever other kind of doomsday Pat Sajak could deal up.

"Care to explain 'getting fancy'?" Junior asked.

"Serena's coming over to help me with some table manners and stuff. Like which fork to use when there's two next to your plate. That's all."

Trent screwed up his face as if they were talking rocket science. "Who cares? All you got to do is just pick up one." He paused, considering. "I mean, as long as it ain't dirty."

Junior nodded. "Why do you need to know about forks, anyway?"

"Because most classy people know about those things."

"Most people don't care," Trent replied. "Not most people I know, anyway."

Though the temptation to tease Trent about the company he kept was strong, Jarred kept the high road. "Serena is going to teach me other stuff, too."

"Such as?"

"Manners. Other stuff…" Because he really didn't know what he needed, just that he needed it something awful, Jarred kept his answer short. "Hell, I don't know. If I knew I wouldn't be hiring her now, would I?"

Trent raised his hands as if he'd just been burned. "Touchy!"

"Shut up. She's due here any minute. When she arrives, y'all need to scoot on out of here. I don't want you getting in the way."

"Not so fast," Trent said. "If Serena's wearing jeans, I could stand around and watch her all day. Maybe I should get some private lessons, too. You, too, Junior."

Junior shook his head. "I'll pass. Serena's great, but I'd rather sit in a ring with a two-ton bull named Damien than talk about forks." Sizing Jarred up, a slow, smooth grin suddenly floated over Junior's face. "Wait a minute, all this is for the auction, isn't it? You're worried about getting an offer."

Trent snapped his fingers. "Don't worry. You won't be a wallflower. I heard the girls at the barbecue joint already talking about bidding all kinds of money for your 'services.' You'll be snapped up."

Jarred winced. Those women at Jim Bob's BBQ were a pushy bunch, and that was the truth. No telling what they'd be having him do for a whole week. He had to spark Veronica's interest. He just had to!

But there was no way he was going to tell them about his infatuation with Veronica Snow. Junior and Trent would start laughing at him and wouldn't know when to stop. "Just the same, I'm going to get a little polish."

He was going to continue some more but the words stuck in his throat when a movement outside the window caught his attention. He shook his head when the ugliest little beat-up sedan, covered in rust and in dire need of a paint job, rolled to a stop in front of their door.

"Man, that's ugly," Junior whispered.

"As ugly as sin," Trent added.

Jarred didn't bother saying any different. That car was ugly, and from the noise the carburetor was making, it wasn't going to make it another six months, neither.

Next to his brothers, Jarred watched Serena Higgens slide out of the driver's side and smooth down her jeans before grabbing her purse. Then she stared at the house and paused… unaware that three sets of eyes were checking her out.

"Lord have mercy," Trent murmured. "I swear those jeans were painted on."

The dark denim did seem to mold to her butt. And the silver concho belt around her hips only served to accentuate her tiny waist.

"I've always been a fan of her hair myself," Junior said. "It's so black and shiny."

For a moment, Jarred also stared at the long swath of hair falling down the middle of her back. Junior did have a point. It looked silky soft. Jarred could only imagine what it looked like in the morning, spread out on her pillows. Or cascading along bare shoulders.

The image was startling and completely unwelcome. "Stop looking at her that way. She's my friend. And now she's even more than that! She's my tutor," Jarred said.

But boy was there a lot to see. Above those jeans was a deceptively plain blue cotton shirt. But the top three buttons were unfastened...just daring a man's eyes to stray there a little longer than was proper.

Finally she moved. When she approached the house, her hips swayed slightly, bringing all attention back to those amazing hips.

Trent whistled low.

Junior blinked, then turned away as if the sight he was seeing was too much for him. "Good luck with your lessons, brother. After I say hi, I'm getting out of here."

"Me, too," Trent said finally. "I think I'll go see if Virginia needs some help getting ready for bed."

When the doorbell rang, Jarred walked across the foyer feeling a little shaky himself. Seeing Serena through his brothers' eyes made him see her in a whole new light.

For a moment, he'd even forgotten Veronica's polished perfection.

An hour ago, he would have never dreamed that was possible.

JARRED'S SMILE WAS A MILE WIDE when he greeted her at his front door. "Hey, Serena. Look at you! You're right on time."

His easy demeanor never failed to bring her up short. Was he joshing her, or genuinely pleased she was punctual? "Hey. I mean, hello. I mean…thank you for seeing me," she stammered as she walked past him into the biggest house she'd ever seen.

Though she'd promised herself she wouldn't look all impressed by his home, she couldn't help it. The foyer was large enough to fit her car in. Maybe two of them. The black-and-white checkered tile floor and spiral staircase in back of it looked old-fashioned in a Hollywood way and was beautiful.

So was the crystal chandelier that hung above their heads, as well as the paintings gracing the dove-gray walls. Both paintings delivered sparks of color and were surprisingly modern.

Though everyone in town had talked about the new Riddell ranch house as being the "cowboy mansion," Serena had privately imagined it looking like something out of a Vegas brothel. This couldn't be more different.

"Your home is beautiful. It's really lovely."

Jarred chuckled as he rocked back on his heels. "You sound surprised."

"I am," she said honestly. "I had imagined something quite different."

"Don't give any of us any credit for it. As first we bought all kinds of rugs and carpets and geegaws. But then one day Gwen said our home looked just like a miniature brothel. And that it was no place for a little girl. So Dad hired a decorator from Dallas."

"She did a good job."

He shrugged. "It's home."

Holding her notepad a little closer to her chest, Serena knew she should say what she'd come to say and get out. Jarred always made her a little nervous—probably because he was just so darn handsome. "Is there somewhere we could talk?"

"Anywhere you want."

Looking beyond him, Serena spotted his two brothers. Though Trent was harmless and Cal. Jr. was a sweetheart, she had no desire to speak frankly in front of them. "Maybe we could go somewhere alone?"

Warily, he looked behind him. Then he glared. "I thought y'all left."

"We were going to…then rethought that plan." Trent sauntered forward. "Hey, Serena. You're looking good. How goes it?"

She couldn't help but smile as he took her hand and kissed her cheek. "I'm just fine, thank you. Surprised to see you. You got a break?"

"Six weeks off. I'm getting into everything around here and messin' stuff up right and left. It's driving Jarred crazy." Leaning closer, he winked. "I hear you're going to make a gentleman out of Jarred."

"I'm going to try," she murmured, though to be honest, she was a little taken aback. She hadn't expected Jarred to already be telling everyone about their plans. "That is, if we can get everything all ironed out."

Still holding her hand, he looked her over in a way that made her feel as if she was something special. "Let me know if you need any help."

"Let me know if he gives you trouble," Cal Jr. drawled. "My older brother doesn't always listen too well to reason."

"I'll keep that in mind."

"Drop her hand, Trent," Jarred said, his voice heavy with irritation. "Drop it and leave."

As soon as Trent did just that, Jarred guided her down the hall. Past the open French doors. Past a humongous dining room and what looked like a butler's pantry and a kitchen decorated in greens and yellows and brick.

Finally, they stopped in a small room near the back of the house. It was glass and shades on three sides and filled with oversize brown wicker furniture. She sat down on a flowery cushion and faced him. "The flowers surprise me. I would never have imagined a room like this in a house full of men."

"We're not all men, remember. Gwen is here, and Ginny, too." Looking at the vase, he smiled. "My mom would have loved this room. She liked to garden and sip her coffee in the morning, watching the birds and such."

"Your mother was a wonderful lady."

"Yes, she was," he said simply.

Finally, they could no longer put off her reason for being there. "So, I'd like to talk to you about charm-school classes. I can only help you if I know exactly what you want to learn."

"I'll tell you what I want to know. But first I think we should talk about what changed your mind."

For a moment, Serena considered keeping the real reason from him. Since he was now living in a house like this, he'd probably forgotten all about trying to stay within the confines of a meager budget.

But pride for her independence trumped her need for privacy. There was nothing wrong with working hard, and nothing wrong with doing her best to help make him a little bit more socially acceptable. "Honestly, it's my bills."

"You got a lot of them?" His eyes turned concerned and his tone gentle.

So gentle that she started telling him more than she'd ever intended to. "I've got more bills than I'm currently able to pay."

"What happened?"

"Life, I guess. The last library levy failed so I got a pay cut. But everything else—college loans, rent, car payments—it all stayed the same."

"I'm sorry."

"Me, too." She wasn't in a position to pretend it didn't matter even though Jarred Riddell probably didn't even remember what it was like to worry about a car payment. "They're becoming overwhelming." Well, they'd become overwhelming about six months ago. Now they were bordering on suffocating.

"So that's why you needed another job."

Serena nodded. "I don't know how much I can help you obtain Veronica's interest. Society life isn't really me, but I'm willing to read as many books as I can to help you out."

He looked at her for a long moment. Really looked. Serena felt his blue eyes skim over her face, take in her outfit, eye her jeans. For a moment doubt settled in, then just as quickly a new resolve entered his expression. "Well, let's get started. Pull out your calendar and let's do some strategizing. We don't have all that much time until the auction. How many lessons do you think I'm going to need to win Veronica over?"

"Maybe two a week?"

"I can do that. How long a session? Maybe an hour?"

She thought quickly. "At least an hour. I've been doing a little bit of reading and came up with some lesson ideas. We'll need to concentrate on all kinds of things, speaking and eating and walking and clothes."

He visibly winced. "That's a lot to remember. Do you think we'll be able to do it all? I'm ashamed to say when I first asked you, I had kind of imagined all you'd need to do was give me a few pointers."

"I'll help you as much as I can, but it isn't going to be easy. It's going to take a lot to catch Veronica's eye. Just think about how unimpressed she was at the Electric Dip. It's going to take hours of effort for her to give you another try."

"I think you might be right."

He looked so bummed, she couldn't help but smile. "Don't worry. I'm going to take these lessons very seriously. If you really want Veronica, then I'll make sure you get her." She pushed a note card his way. "What do you think about tackling these things first off?"

Jarred looked at the class descriptions and scowled. "Walking and opening doors? Come on, Serena. I'm crude, not completely useless."

"The books say you're doing it all wrong, though. I promise I'm right about this. If we're going to polish you up, it's going to take some time. We can't just do it halfway."

He put down the card with a sigh. "All right. I'll give you two one-hour sessions a week."

"Will the evenings work for you? I have to work at the library during the day, you know."

"I can fit you in. Now we ought to talk money. What do you think sounds fair? A hundred dollars an hour?"

Even though both of them knew she was only helping him because she needed the money, Serena still felt uncomfortable. It felt wrong to help him for so much.

But only a payment as exorbitant as that would get her out of financial hot water. "That amount sounds fair to me."

He snapped his fingers. "I just had an idea."

"What is that?"

"I'll give you an additional thousand-dollar bonus if Veronica bids on me."

"Bids and wins or just bids?"

"Bids high enough to win. What do you say?"

"I say why not? I know she's going to find you irresistible real soon."

"You sound awfully sure about that."

"That's because I am." Serena willed herself to sound businesslike. To her, Jarred Riddell had always been appealing. He was handsome and happy. He was kind but had just enough of a devilish charm to make her knees melt.

He stood up. "So, we'll start in two days?"

"Yes. I'll see you on Thursday evening. At seven."

"I'll be ready, too, darling," he said as he walked her back to the front door. "I'll be ready and willing. I promise."

His look of promise was so gorgeous, Serena almost forgot that she was only doing it for the money.

Chapter Six

"Hannah, there's no doubt about it. I'm absolutely the dumbest woman in Texas," Serena said on Thursday morning when she joined her assistant in the library's back storage room.

Pushing her peacock-blue reading glasses down her nose, Hannah shot a curious glance her way. "I find that hard to believe."

"It's true. I'm plain dumb."

"That may be, but Texas is a mighty big state. There's got to be someone dumber. Maybe out by Amarillo?"

Serena was so taken aback by the complete lack of sympathy, she burst out laughing. "Thanks for that. For a moment, I was getting so stressed out, I thought I was going to have an aneurism or something."

After placing a few more sets of markers, paper clips and folders on her cart, Hannah turned to her. "What's wrong? Is the city getting miserly with our funding again?"

"No, it's nothing like that. It's of a more personal nature."

"Then it can only do with one man."

"Yep." Unable to help herself, Serena scowled. "I just got off the phone with Jarred. We're meeting this evening and I told him he needed to wear some dress shoes and a blazer. He said he didn't own either. How can that even be possible?

He's rich! Plus, I know he goes out for steak at the Cattleman's Club. They've got a dress code there, I'm sure of it."

"So what did you say?"

"I said he better make a trip to the city this afternoon and pick one out." Just remembering their exchange made Serena get all riled up again. "Of course, he told me that wasn't going to happen anytime soon."

"Maybe you shouldn't be expecting him to wear different clothes," Hannah said slowly. "You have to admit, there never has been anything wrong with the way Jarred looks. Actually, he's so fine, I'd be real reluctant to cover him up with anything."

"His Lucchese boots have never bothered me, either," Serena admitted. "But Veronica Snow is going to want more than a rough-around-the-edges guy. And Jarred's paying me good money to transform him into the kind of man she wants. So he needs to listen to what I say."

Leading the way out of the stuffy stockroom, Hannah looked over her shoulder as she pushed the cart. "Are you sure Veronica wants Jarred in a blazer? I'd prefer him barechested myself."

Resolutely, Serena pushed all images of a half-naked Jarred out of her head. She imagined Jarred, all tanned torso, would be a mighty fine thing…but not for the ladies who wrote the etiquette books she'd been staying up late reading.

She cleared her throat. "Boots and bare chests aren't classy."

As they walked down the empty corridor toward the nonfiction stacks, Hannah's voice echoed after her. "You know, there is that old saying about how clothes make a man. I think it's probably real true in Jarred's case."

"This time, I think that saying's flawed. Clothes don't actually make a person. But the right kind of clothes are going to catch Veronica's eye. You've seen how she dresses—it's all designery and pretty."

Her lips twitching, Hannah looked over at Serena. "I know it's the opposite of your, um, style."

Serena felt her cheeks heat. While it was true she couldn't help but wear her usual uniform of jeans and boots, she also had a feeling she'd never look as good as Veronica did in her slim-fitting short skirts and silk blouses. "Just because I don't dress up like Veronica doesn't mean I haven't been studying her type. I went out and bought copies of *Town & Country* and *InStyle* magazines last night."

Before Hannah could say a word about that, Serena continued. "Anyway, Jarred's going to have to wear a tuxedo at the auction. At the moment, I don't think he's ever worn anything but flip-flops, boots or tennis shoes."

"You sound very prepared for tonight's lesson."

"I think I am." Thinking of the many note cards and lists she'd made up the evening before, Serena squared her shoulders. "We're going to get him completely transformed if he'll mind me."

"Oh, my. I hope you know what you're doing."

"You're forgetting, Hannah. This wasn't my idea. He's the one who wants to change. I'm just the transformer."

"You're right. I keep forgetting that. Well, best of luck to you, then."

Eager to think about something else besides Jarred, Serena slipped on her glasses. "What's on our agenda today?"

"Schoolchildren, budget meetings and ordering."

"Sounds like my kind of day. There will be people to read to, complain about and commiserate with."

"My sentiments exactly." Pointing to the glass-enclosed office, Hannah said, "The first group of students arrives in two hours. Go work on those orders, Miss Higgens."

"I will, gladly."

EIGHT HOURS LATER, SERENA would have paid money to deal only with a class of fidgeting six-year-olds. They were easier than the man in front of her.

From the moment he'd entered the library, he'd been cutting up something awful. "Jarred, it's bad enough that you came in here with dirty boots and dusty clothes instead of the shoes and blazer I told you to. But now you aren't even trying to listen to a thing I say."

"I'm listening," he retorted, though he didn't look as if he was. In fact, he seemed more interested in the variety of cookbooks on the shelf behind him than anything else in the room. Slipping one off the shelf, he opened it up. "By the way, have you ever made a thirty-minute meal?"

In spite of herself, Serena found herself looking at the Rachael Ray cookbook, too. "No."

"This Rachael, she's a real spitfire, I'll tell you that. See, she's got a cashew chicken recipe that's to die—"

"Jarred, put that book down." When he complied, she pointed across the room to her office door. "One more time, you need to practice entering a room with a lady."

Obediently, he marched back to the glass door. "Come on, then." He tapped his boot as she walked over to his side. "Lord, but you're slow."

Resolutely ignoring him, Serena flashed a smile instead. "Jarred, it's so nice to see you. Are you ready to go inside?"

"I've been ready."

Pointedly, she looked at the door. With a scowl, he twisted the handle and opened it, then stepped right in front of her—effectively blocking her way.

"You have to open it and then stand to the side, so I can walk through," she explained.

"That's kind of hard to do. My arms aren't six feet long."

"You're impossible. Switch places with me."

"What?"

"Get over here," she directed. "Now, take ten steps backward and pretend you're me."

He did as she directed, then sauntered close, batting his eyelashes. "Hi. I'm here."

She rolled her eyes. "Yes, you are. And you look so nice this evening, Jarred. I...uh, like your—" Frantically, she looked for something to compliment him on. Since his jeans were faded and molded to his very fine legs and the T-shirt had a beer ad on it, both of those articles were out of the question. The only thing left was the shiny buckle glinting at her in silver splendor. "Your, um, belt buckle."

"Thanks. I won that in Wyoming two years ago. That bull was a mean SOB, I'll tell you that." His smile turned languid as he stepped a bit closer. "'Course, I never imagined you'd be the kind of girl to be inspecting my nether regions."

"That's exactly the kind of thing you shouldn't be saying."

"Well, I don't think it's very ladylike for you to be looking at me down there."

"It's hard to ignore! That buckle is gold and silver and huge!"

"Oh, darling, it's nothing."

Face flaming, she sidestepped, opened the door with one hand, then stepped out of the way. "Enter."

He did as she asked.

After she closed the door behind her, Serena did a little bow. "That, Jarred, is how you were supposed to do it."

"Do what?"

"Open the door for a woman."

"Oh, hell, Serena, I wasn't paying a lick of attention to how you stepped around. We better do it again."

Serena's temper was boiling. Barely reining in her irritation, she retraced her steps, then held the door open for him again. "Now it's your turn."

Finally listening, he opened the door, sidestepped a bit so she could walk through, then led her into her office.

"That was much better."

"I know." He yawned. "I don't know about you, but I'm ready for a break."

She looked at the clock on the wall. "We can't stop, we just got started."

"Come on. All you've been doing is complaining and nagging me. Let's stop early for the night."

Crossing to her desk, she picked up the note cards she'd worked on for a solid hour before he showed up late. "We've only gotten a fourth of the way through with my plans. We were going to tackle opening car doors and walking side by side on the sidewalk."

"Are you serious? I know how to walk."

"Not with a lady. Now, you stand here a sec and watch me walk." She took a few steps in front of him, just so he would get the idea. Over her shoulder, she called out, "Do you notice how my steps aren't near as big as yours?"

"Kind of."

His voice sounded kind of hoarse. Almost strained. "Oh, for heaven's sakes. Watch me again." She took another five steps forward, then turned around. "Now, I know I just have on jeans and boots, but you can imagine how I might look with something else on."

"Oh, honey. I can imagine."

Confused, she met his gaze. Jarred was looking at her as though she was practically a stranger. "Are you okay?"

"I'm good. I'm just a little warm." Stepping backward, he mumbled, "I need to be getting on my way. Now."

"But—"

His eyes hardened. "Look, if it will make you feel any better, I'll pay you for the whole time." He pulled out his wallet from his back pocket and deftly handed over a hundred-dollar bill. "Take it or leave it. I'm done."

Serena knew her face was flaming as she took the money. Deftly, she slipped it into her back pocket. "Thank you." To her surprise, Jarred watched her every move.

He pulled on his T-shirt's collar. "No problem. I've got to get going."

She followed him out to the book stacks back out to where he'd left his hat. "But we're not done. Please stay."

His gaze flickered over her blouse, to where it opened on her chest. "Sorry, Serena. But it's just too damn hot in here. I mean, really."

Before she could comment on that, he pivoted and left the library, barely forty-five minutes after he'd entered.

Staring at the hundred-dollar bill, Serena fought back the bitter taste in her mouth. She'd just taken money for accomplishing nothing.

Though a tiny part of her said she should be celebrating—now she could pay her student loan on time—Serena couldn't help but feel like a huge failure.

She'd just sunk to a new low.

And what was worse, she was already looking forward to seeing him again.

Chapter Seven

When Jarred met his brother on the sidewalk in front of Ed's Feed and Seed at four o'clock the next day, Junior looked him up and down. Then he spit. "So, you charming yet?"

Even though Jarred was standing straight and proud in front of his F-150, inside he was squirming. His brother was making him feel as if he was less on the ball than he'd originally thought.

He was probably right about that, too.

"Maybe."

"You don't know? I would have thought you'd have some idea."

"Me, too," Jarred replied as they walked inside the feed store. As the unmistakable smell of the hundred-year-old store surrounded them—really, nothing could ever match the pungent scent of Ed's in the spring—he dropped off their latest order for oats and grain. "Do you think y'all can fill this pretty soon?"

"Most likely," Ed said as he keyed it into the computer, looking at them only when it was time to hand over a credit card. "That it, boys?" he asked around a wad of Bazooka gum.

"Almost," Junior replied. "We'll need a six-pack of antibiotic bottles for the calves, too."

Ed chomped. "They're in the refrigerated case. You go get 'em."

As soon as Junior set the six-pack in the cooler in his truck bed, he motioned toward the diner down the street. "That Ed. He's going to be asking how 'we boys' are when we're sixty-five."

Jarred grinned. "And he'll still be asking it around a wad of gum—if his jaw still works."

"Want to grab a burger?"

"Always."

As the noon sun burned down on their shoulders and they wandered along the beat-up sidewalk, Junior looked his way again. "So you really think you need these manners classes?"

"If I want Veronica, I do."

"Mmm. So how did it go last night?"

"Not too bad."

Of course, he hadn't been too good, either.

Jarred knew he'd been brash enough to deserve a licking from his momma. She would have boxed his ears good if she'd been standing in that library, watching him give Serena such a hard time.

But no way was he going to let on any of that to his brother. "It lasted forever," he said cockily. "I could hardly wait to leave." Then, in an all-out effort to save face, he added, "Plus, that class was a bust."

But instead of grinning at his misbehavior, Junior looked kind of worried as they stepped around a pair of ladies shopping at the dollar sidewalk sale. "What was wrong?" he asked. "You couldn't do all the things Serena wanted you to?"

"I could. Well, almost." Thinking about their time together, thinking about how his eyes started drifting to the way her butt looked sashaying away from him…Jarred frowned. "I could do the things that were worthwhile. Not the idiotic stuff."

"Like what?"

Jarred demonstrated by stepping to the next entry and opening the door to the Hallmark store. "Things like this."

"Like what?"

Just as Junior was staring at him in confusion, old Mrs. Crane walked right through that open door with a smile on her face. "Why, thank you, Jarred. That's so kind of you."

"You're welcome, ma'am," he said before meeting Junior back on the sidewalk. When they were out of earshot, he scratched his head. "Huh. Maybe opening doors for women works."

"Mrs. Crane sure liked it."

Then, to Jarred's dismay, when cute Mrs. Fuller, their former English teacher, approached, Junior darted to the door and opened it for her.

Just like a trained seal.

Mrs. Fuller smiled broadly. "Oh, thank you, Cal. What a sweetie you've become!"

He tipped his hat. "Ma'am." After he closed the door, Junior looked at him and winked. "Worked like a charm."

"Heck, yeah." But though his voice was sure, inside Jarred knew it was all bravado. His little brother was making that little lesson look like the easiest thing imaginable. He, on the other hand, hadn't been able to do half as well with a whole lot more instruction.

And then he'd started thinking that maybe Junior had it right when he'd said her dark hair was real pretty.

And then he'd begun itching to place his hands on those denim-clad hips and hold her close…and he'd practically gone crazy, he'd been so mad at himself.

So he acted like a jerk and ran out of there. That was embarrassing.

Electra was busy. Most everyone they knew was either walking or driving by. As they continued the last three blocks to the restaurant, it became a full-time occupation to either wave or say hey to everyone who passed.

And then they ran into Veronica Snow.

"Excuse me," she murmured when he'd been standing flat in the middle of the sidewalk talking to his brother, effectively blocking everyone's way coming and going.

Abruptly, he straightened. "Huh?"

Junior grabbed his arm and jerked hard to the left. "We're in the way, stupid." Smiling sweetly her way, he said, "Sorry. Are you going in the pharmacy?"

"Yes." She looked almost apologetic. "My mother needed some prescriptions filled."

While Jarred stood there motionless, Junior—the snake—hopped right over and opened that pharmacy door for her. "She doing poorly?" he asked.

"No worse than usual." A wan smile peeked out. "Some days are just tough, you know?" Then her cell phone chirped, she pasted it to her ear, and with a little wave of thanks, crossed the threshold.

Meanwhile, the wide-open door was cooling their area of the sidewalk. The manager of the pharmacy was motioning for them to get in or shut the door.

More people were walking by.

Veronica paused and stared at him. "Hold on," she told whoever was on the phone…then looked back at him. "Did you need something?"

Say something, he told himself. *Say something. Anything!*

"We needed medicine for our cows," he blurted.

Wide blue eyes snapped to his, then narrowed. "I hope they feel better," she said before sticking that phone back to her ear and walking into the store.

Junior punched his shoulder. Hard. "Cows?"

"What was wrong with that?"

"You just compared her mother's illness with a couple of colicky calves, that's what's wrong."

"They're sick, too."

To his surprise, Junior hit him again. "Whatever you're paying Serena, it's not enough. You're a wreck, Jarred. That Veronica Snow is never going to pay good money for your time."

"She will. I know she will."

"She's not. She's never going to like you. Hell, she's never going to give you the time of day."

"Sure she is. Just as soon as I finish my lessons with Serena."

"Good luck with that," Junior said with a snort.

"Knowing how to hold the door open for a lady doesn't mean squat."

"It does to me. You suck at it."

"I'm getting better."

As they entered the Burger Shack, Junior held the door open for two more girls. Just as if it was his new trick.

When the teenagers giggled and sputtered thanks, Junior tipped his hat at them and grinned evilly at him.

"Shut up and buy me a burger," Jarred said as he grabbed a table by the front window.

As Junior walked away, laughing, Jarred knew his brother was right. He needed another lesson. And he needed it fast.

Pulling out his cell phone, he dialed Serena's number.

After listening to some sappy Shania Twain song, her voice mail clicked on. "Please leave me a message."

Jarred didn't waste time with pleasantries. "Serena, here's the thing. I need another lesson. Fast. Can you fit me in tonight? I'll pay double." He paused. "And, uh, I promise I'll behave better, too. Call me."

He slipped the phone into his pocket just as his brother appeared with two tall glasses of iced tea.

There was no way Junior was going to get the better of him with this manners stuff. No way. No how.

THE BANK WAS CROWDED. She waited in line as patiently as she could, all the while trying to avoid eye contact with Pete Ross in his office. Soon after she'd entered the bank building, the couple he was meeting with left. Through his glass door, she watched him shuffle papers around. Then he looked up and caught sight of her.

"Shoot," she moaned.

The man in front of her turned around and glared. Serena glared right back. And then pasted a pleasant smile on her face the moment she smelled Pete's overpowering cologne. Aqua Velva.

"Whatcha doing here, Serena?"

He always drew out her name, making it sound almost four syllables. She supposed the habit would be a catchy thing if she thought it sounded good on his lips. But it didn't. Didn't at all. Perhaps it was his New England–transplant voice. The kind of nasal sound that no amount of enforced twang could fix. He wasn't Texan, and that was a fact.

"Just waiting in line. You know. Doing my thing."

He leaned a little closer. "You got some time for a cup of coffee?"

"Oh, gee. Thanks, but I should get going."

"Maybe another time, then."

"Yes. Definitely." The line moved. She stepped forward. Now there were just four in front of her. Hopefully, their business would go fast and she could get out of there.

"Or…we could go to dinner?"

It took a little doing, but she was able to adopt a regretful expression real fast. "I don't know. I'm working an awful lot right now."

"At the library?"

"And other places." Oh, why wouldn't that darn line move fast? "I've taken a part-time job."

"What for?"

As the man in front of her turned around, obviously eavesdropping for all he was worth, Serena felt her cheeks heat. "Bills."

He curved a soft hand around her elbow. His expression was earnest. "Why don't you come into my office and we'll talk?"

"I don't have time—"

"But I could help. I am a financial analyst, too, you know."

She knew he cared. He really did. But she didn't want anything to do with him. Not in that way. Instinctively, she knew she'd be beholden to him. "Not today," she said firmly.

"Hey, Pete?" One of the girls in the back was staring at him, her arms crossing her chest. "You got a client waiting."

"Think about it, Serena. Will you?"

"Oh, yes," she lied.

After a reassuring squeeze, he walked away. She breathed a sigh of relief, just as the man in line turned around. For a third time. "You should have gone, little lady. That guy knows what he's talking about."

"Maybe you should mind your own business."

"I CAN'T BELIEVE I'M DOING this. I can't believe I took pity on you and agreed to help you tonight," Serena said the moment Jarred entered the library at seven-fifteen. "After the way you cut up the other day, I shouldn't even have returned your call."

"I'm glad you did. I was desperate."

"What about?" She looked at him a little more closely. Once she got over his fine features and gorgeous physique, she had to admit that he looked a bit…blue. "Hey…are you okay?"

"I'm fine." He looked at the floor. "It's nothing of consequence. Now let's get started. I've got things to do."

That set her off. Serena figured if she was going to reschedule her girls' night out with Tracy at the last minute, she ought to at least have gotten a good explanation. "Well, just so you know, I have other things I could be doing, too. Plus, you got here late."

"I'm not that late. Not by much."

"Anything counts." Though she knew her voice had taken on a schoolmarm edge, she tapped her toe. "You know, being on time shows you care about a person."

With a scowl, Jarred pulled out a fancy silver cell phone that looked as if it cost more than her food budget for the whole month. Flipping it open, he scanned the time. "I'm barely fifteen minutes late."

"That's a big problem."

"Being late?"

"Of course. It shows the other person that you don't care enough about them. That you only care about yourself."

"Hold on. Most girls are never ready on time anyway." He looked around the library in a vague way. "I figured you'd still be doing whatever librarians do."

"I was waiting for you. That's what I was doing." Oh, but he annoyed her like no other. Did he really think all she did all day was sit around and wait for him? And work?

"Whatever. Just add it to the bill."

She was tempted. But after pocketing his money last time for lessons never covered, Serena was afraid to accept. She went on the offensive instead. "I should probably tell you that I read online today that most gentlemen wear watches."

Jarred sat down on the flimsy plastic orange chair opposite. "Is that right?"

"Uh-huh." Recalling the blurb, she recited it from memory. "'Most well-dressed gentlemen favor a fine timepiece. Since it's usually their only piece of jewelry, it says a lot about them.'" Serena cleared her throat. "It also makes it easier to keep track of time. And you won't be constantly pulling that phone out of your jeans."

"There's nothing wrong with that."

"Sure there is. Whenever I watch you pull that cell phone out, I'm sure you're checking texts or missed calls. And that won't do."

His lips twitched. "It won't?"

"No, it won't. I'm right about this, Jarred. I know it."

For a moment, she was sure he was going to argue. Serena wouldn't have been surprised—pointing out the fact that he needed a timepiece did sound a little nitpicky, even to her ears. "Actually, I was thinking maybe I did need to get me one of those Submariners."

"A what?"

"One of those Rolexes that you can take deep-sea diving," he casually explained. "They're cool."

It was on the tip of her tongue to ask how in the heck he planned to go scuba diving in north Texas, but decided to use a little of the positive reinforcement she'd read about, too. "That's a real fine idea."

Jarred looked pleased.

"Let's move on. Cell phones and watches weren't on the agenda."

"What is?"

"Errands. When I started thinking about the kinds of things you might be doing with Veronica, I realized it might be beneficial to think about the proper way to behave when y'all are out running errands."

He blinked before slipping into a very sexy smile. "I don't think she's going to want me for errands, Serena."

"But—" She stopped herself just in time. Unbidden images of Jarred removing that too-big belt buckle appeared and no matter how hard she tried to dispel the picture, it was firmly entrenched in her head. "I thought you said you weren't aiming to sleep with her."

"I said I wasn't going to *gigolo* myself," he slyly corrected. "However, taking her to bed when the time is right is definitely not going to be a problem."

Serena imagined it wouldn't. Once again that belt buckle shined in her head, making her think of Jarred wearing a whole lot less than what he had on at the moment.

She cleared her throat. "Um. However…just in case she's not ready for bed right away, you need some help." She gave him a sharp glare. "That's what you're paying me for, right?"

"Right. I need your help for when we're out and about in town. I won't need any tips for when Veronica and I are alone. I promise, no one's ever complained about my behavior in the bedroom."

"No, I imagine not." Mouth dry, she glanced up at the clock on the wall—7:25. They'd just spent the past ten interminable minutes discussing cell phones and his expertise in bed.

She was getting mighty uncomfortable and terribly jealous, and he'd gotten nowhere closer to being a gentleman, and now she was reduced to wondering just how skilled he was in the bedroom.

Well, there was only one remedy for that—and it was to keep things purely professional. "Stand up, let's get started."

He stood and followed her to a round table with four items on it. An umbrella, a shopping bag with five books, a linen handkerchief and a lady's coat. "What's all this for?"

"I'm going to teach you what to do with all of it."

He picked up the handkerchief and promptly shook it open. "I already know how to blow my nose."

"Emily Post says every gentleman needs to carry a handkerchief."

After he folded it up, he stuffed it in his back pocket. "Now what?"

Serena had been thinking long and hard about how to train Jarred, and she'd decided that the only way to make sure he could do things was to playact situations. "Let's pretend I'm crying. What do you do?"

He looked at her a good long time. Then, just like a tiger pouncing on its prey, he strode forward, folded his arms around her and held her close. Real close. So close that her nose was smooshed up against his chest and she could barely breathe.

Heat radiated from the cotton fabric of his T-shirt. So did his scent. That wonderful, tangy Armani and man-smell that made her insides melt and her brain turn to mush.

With supreme effort, she focused. Just when she was about to tell him that gentlemen did not grab their women and plaster them against their bodies, one of those amazing, almost too big, roughed up, incredibly masculine hands patted her head... and then drifted to her back.

Then her lower back.

Then settled on her...rear end?

"There, there, honey. Stop crying, now," he crooned, patting her butt. "You know how I hate to see you cry."

Even though she knew they were just pretending. Even though she knew he'd never thought of her as anything more than just his pal...it was as if her body had never gotten that memo. In short order, her knees went limp. Her body felt languid as she pressed a little closer to him. Hips pressed against his. Her breasts flattened against his chest.

Yes, her body felt just right.

He let out a little groan as his hands readjusted themselves again, cupping her rear.

She knew she should stop him.

She knew she should tell him that it wasn't good manners to grab girls' rears and hold on tight. But she couldn't do it. All she really wanted to do was slide her face to the left, press her cheek on his chest and breathe in his scent.

And so she did. Once again, their bodies adjusted to each other. One of his hands glided up her spine, gently caressing her. Under her ear, she could hear his heartbeat. Steady. Sure. Her hands itched to move. To circle around his neck. To pull his head down. Just a little. Just enough for her to look up and brush his lips with her own.

Just for a second….

A little shudder dragged through him. "Serena, are you done crying yet?" he asked, his voice strained.

"Y-yes." Her head popped up. She knew her face was flushed. She knew she was aroused—and Lord have mercy— she knew he was, too. With as much dignity as she could muster, she stepped back. "Perhaps we should move on. I think you can comfort a woman just fine, though maybe with Veronica you could offer her a handkerchief. She'd probably appreciate that."

"Would you?"

She shrugged. "We, uh, can't always judge my reaction to you as the best course. I'm not fancy like Veronica."

"You may not be fancy, but you're sure pretty."

She blinked. She couldn't remember another time when Jarred had ever noticed. "Thank you. Now, let's work on another prop."

He picked up the umbrella and he twirled it a bit, like a clumsy Gene Kelly. "What's this for? Rain?"

"Obviously," she said tartly. "But what it's really for is to remind you that if it's raining, you need to open it for her, and then hold the umbrella over her head. Even if it means you might get wet."

"I'm seriously paying you money to learn this?"

"Of course."

"It doesn't sound too hard."

"I don't think so, either. But Miss Manners says there's a certain skill to it. We better practice."

His blue eyes twinkled. "How are we going to pretend rain, Serena? Get in the shower?"

There went that image again. Jarred. Naked. Wet. Hot. Perfect. She cleared her throat and tried to concentrate on bills. Lots of bills.

"I'm going to sit down," she said. "You're going to need to pretend you're opening my car door."

"Uh-huh." It really was amazing how much disbelief Jarred could squeeze out of that utterance.

"And while you do that, hold out the umbrella for me."

"It hasn't rained in Electra in months."

She sat. "When it does, you'll be ready. Now get started."

Loping over, he pretended to open a car door, then looked up at the library's ceiling with wide eyes. "My word! It's raining! Looky here, Serena, I just happened to have an umbrella with me, too."

Before she could critique him, he pointed the umbrella her way, pushed the button, and the thing sprang to action in an instant. So fast, that the nylon brushed her face and only her quick reflexes enabled her to jerk to the right.

Those reflexes didn't prevent her from falling over, however.

She groaned in frustration. "Jarred! You almost took my eye out."

"Crap. Get up, Serena. I'm getting rained on, here."

"Hold out your hand so I can take it."

He held out a hand. "Jeez, I never knew you were so helpless."

Taking his hand, she glared up at him through the sharp metal points of the umbrella. The same points that kept threatening to poke her again, he was so incredibly clumsy. "It doesn't matter if I can do something or not. You're supposed to *want* to help me." When he still didn't look as though he had a clue, she huffed. "Pretend I'm Veronica!"

Gently, he ran a thumb over her knuckles, then pulled her up. "Better?" he murmured.

"Better," she said as she tried hard to ignore the little zing of tension that sprang to life between them.

"Now hold up the umbrella so I can get under it."

Without a word, he repositioned the umbrella with his left hand, still holding her hand with his right. He stepped closer. Her shoulders brushed against his raised arm. They shifted. Now her chest touched his. Again.

And then, for the second time in five minutes, Serena found herself enveloped by his scent. And that body of hers— dammit! That body sidled up next to him just as if they'd been made for each other.

Her breath caught. Her mouth went dry. Then she made the lethal mistake of looking into his eyes. Right then and there, she was a goner.

"Damn," he breathed, right before he bent down and brushed his lips against hers.

Unable to stop herself, she lifted her head, tilted it to one side and kissed him again. His lips were firm and cool. But there was an awareness there. Slowly, their lips met one more time, lips slightly parted. Still chaste—so chaste, but they lingered. Savoring. It would be so easy to open a little wider. To finally taste him….

But wait. He was pretending she was someone else. With a jerk, she stepped back. "That's it. You did good," she croaked. "I mean well." Her cheeks burned. "I mean fine. You did fine. Veronica would, um, have no complaint there."

His eyes clouded, surely mirroring what had to be going on with her own. "Good. I mean, I'm glad I figured that out."

Before she could reply to that—not that she had anything worthwhile to say—Jarred handed her the umbrella.

Their fingers brushed. He pulled his fingers away as if they'd been singed, and stepped away from her side in such a hurry you'd have thought she had the plague.

'Course she did feel feverish. But he'd always had that effect on her. She struggled to get them back on track. "So, now we could probably work on helping a lady with a jacket."

His eyes darted to the table of props, then back to hers.

Serena's mouth went dry as she imagined him slipping his hands over her shoulders. Stepping close to him again. Oh, Lord.

"Or, we could tackle that another time?"

"I think another time's best. Um, Serena, I know I said this was an emergency and all…but maybe we could stop? I'm sorry, but I think I've had enough."

She'd had enough, too. Enough of thinking about him in ways that she wasn't supposed to. All she was going to do was hurt herself. They had no future. And never would.

"That would be best."

He grabbed his hat, the Stetson that he'd tossed on the front table when he entered. "See you in three days?"

"Three days is fine."

After another long look her way, his lips parted as though he was trying to find the right words but coming up empty-handed, he turned and walked out.

When the door swooshed closed behind him, Serena sat down with a sigh. Tutoring him was just as terrible as she'd feared it was going to be. When she was around Jarred, she imagined herself more than she was—and realized she was so much less than what she'd dreamed she could be.

Standing under that umbrella had brought back memories

of high school, back when they'd had lockers near each other. Every morning, he'd say hi with a little grin, ask how she was doing.

And then after a pat on the shoulder or a lazy grin, he'd move on to other things.

Mainly flirting with everyone else. Even back then, she'd gotten jealous.

Of course, he'd never even realized it. Each day she'd watch the popular girls circle him like pretty vultures, waiting to be noticed. And more often than not, he'd noticed every one of them. He'd never said much to her—well, there had been the time when she'd been running for high-school treasurer and he'd asked her why she'd even wanted to run.

She'd been so flustered, she'd told him she didn't know. He'd said that was a real shame.

Chapter Eight

Jarred knew he was acting like a fool, but ever since he'd seen Veronica buying ice cream at the Electric Dip, he'd taken to stopping by there on a regular basis. Just for a look-see.

Usually, he'd just miss her. Paula would fill him in on little details about Veronica's purchase or comment on what she was wearing. He'd collect the information for later use.

By now, he knew she drove a pretty little cream-colored Lincoln, liked to eat ice cream almost daily…and that she favored anything sweet that had next to zero calories.

Just when he'd given up catching a glimpse of her for the day, Jarred saw Veronica sitting with Hannah at one of the back tables with just about the biggest dish of chocolate-fudge ice cream Paula offered.

From the looks of things, Hannah was doing all the talking and Veronica was doing all the eating. A lot.

The mound of chocolate was half-gone, and from the looks of the intent expression on her face, Veronica was well on her way to joining the clean-plate club.

Something was obviously terribly wrong.

Before she had a crisis of conscience and threw the rest of that dish of decadence out, he swerved into a parking lot, kicked on his Ford's parking brake, then tipped his hat back on his head and ambled her way.

"Hey, Hannah. Veronica," he drawled as soon as the women turned his way.

"Hi there, Jarred," Hannah said. "Care to join us? We're just trying to keep cool."

"I swear, I can't think of anything I'd rather do," he said quickly.

Veronica said nothing, simply stared at him, spoon in her mouth.

For a moment, he thought about those lips of hers. But, with a shock, all he was able to do was think about how sweet Serena's lips were when he'd kissed her. Straddling the chair across from Veronica, he fought to stay on target. "Looks like you're having quite a treat today."

"I am."

When she said nothing more and Hannah just tittered, he brought out the charm. "It looks good. Real good." Her eyes widened. He grinned. Yes, there was a double entendre there. Damn, he was awesome.

"It's terrific. I couldn't resist getting a big bowl of chocolate Turtles decadence. I'm probably going to gain ten pounds."

"That is a king-size helping. Probably enough for two." Though, as soon as the lame joke left his mouth, he was filled with regret. Hannah glared.

Oops. He knew better. Even his brothers could have told him not to tease a woman about her eating habits. "Not that there's anything wrong with liking big portions."

"Oh, there is." With a look of displeasure, Veronica pushed the dish a few inches away, though Jarred noticed that she didn't let go of the spoon. "I don't usually eat stuff like this. It's just been one of those days."

"I've had days like that, too," he ventured, hardly able to believe that they were sitting together, having a nice conversation.

"Really?" Hannah asked. "Do tell."

Now things felt awkward. It was nearly impossible to flirt with Veronica while Hannah sat there.

And almost impossible to flirt with a woman who seemed far more interested in ingesting empty calories than catching all his flirtatious ways.

But he was determined to try his best. "'Course, my vices run more toward tequila. If I were you, I'd be proud of your ice-cream weakness. No matter how much you eat, you can still drive home."

She brightened a bit. "I hadn't thought about it like that."

"Well, then, thank goodness I just happened to stop by," he said with a smile—just in case she thought it was strange he stopped by her table at all.

Ever so slowly, she pulled her dish closer and dipped that spoon into the bowl again, almost as though she couldn't stop herself.

Her temptation made him smile. Maybe she wasn't too perfect after all.

Because there was no time like the present to set a person's mind to motion, he said, "Say, have you heard about the upcoming community auction?"

After licking her spoon clean, she replied. "I have."

"Are you planning to go? I hear it's going to be a real humdinger."

"I wouldn't miss it for the world."

Now that sounded encouraging. "Is that right?"

"Oh, yes."

Jarred watched her ice cream melt in the heat…and temptation light up her eyes one more time. "Ice cream's melting, sweetheart."

She swiped at the spoon with her tongue.

As he watched—completely mesmerized—Veronica kept licking and talking. "Actually, I used to plan social events like that back in Dallas. I was pretty good at it, too, if I do say so myself."

After she rambled on for another minute or two, Veronica paused. "You didn't know how important designer contributions are to bridal fundraisers?"

"No," he murmured. "I mean, I'm real impressed with your…work ethic. You seem very capable."

"Why, thank you."

"I meant to say, I think you're pretty incredible, if you don't mind me saying. You're so beautiful. And, um…smart."

"Why, thank you, Jarred. That's so sweet! And kind. It's not every man who can appreciate why it's so important to me to take shopping trips to Dallas."

That was him—Mr. Kindness. Eager to steer the conversation to the auction, and to him, he asked, "Since we're discussing auctions and all, I was wondering… Have you ever bid on anything good?"

"I certainly have." She leaned forward. Touched his forearm with two pink polished nails. "Jarred, are you planning to attend?"

Nerves and pride and cockiness made him reply with something a little bit more than was necessary. "Darling, I'm doing more than that. I'm part of it."

Her pretty smile faltered. "How so?"

"I'm auctioning myself off. As a date for a whole week." Unable to stop himself, he winked and puffed out his chest. Might as well give her a good sample of what was in store for her.

Shoot, maybe this whole winning over Veronica Snow was going to be easier than he'd thought after all. Maybe he could stop the foolish lessons with Serena and simply concentrate on winning Veronica's heart, like he'd hoped to do from the first time he'd set eyes on her.

"A whole week. With you. My, that's very interesting."

Something in her voice told him that she wasn't near as impressed with the idea as he'd anticipated. "I think it's incredible, too."

"I see."

Her extreme lack of excitement was taking the wind right out of his sails. "I am something of a catch, you know," he said, and just in case she was thinking he was too full of himself, he added, "Right, Hannah?"

Hannah rolled her eyes.

He soldiered on. "People asked me to do this. To auction myself off. It wasn't my idea."

"No, I imagine it wasn't."

Huh?

As if the Lord above him was monitoring their conversation, a sharp rumble of thunder grumbled overhead.

Veronica looked up with some concern and—was that relief he spied in her eyes, too? "Oh, my," she gasped. "I didn't even notice the clouds roll in. It looks like rain."

"Maybe, but I doubt it."

"I better go." Looking embarrassed, she fingered one of the sleeves to her white cotton top. "I sure don't want to get caught in a storm with just this on."

"No, I imagine you wouldn't. That's a real sheer little top you got on. A little bit of rain would make it transparent."

"Jarred," Hannah warned.

Veronica looked Hannah's way and stood up. "I really better go."

"No, wait!" he barked out. If he let this opportunity with Veronica pass him by, he'd be up a creek, for sure. "You've still got a bit of chocolate left in that bowl. Might as well finish it. It ain't gonna rain."

Hannah kicked him. "Let her go, Jarred."

But somehow, he couldn't. "You know, us cowboys know a

thing or two about cloud formations and forecasting weather the old-fashioned way. I know what I'm talking about."

Down went her arms. "I suppose you would. I think my mother said you were a rodeo star or something like that. I guess you would know a thing or two about nature."

"Oh, I do, honey. I know a lot about nature," he drawled. "I've spent more hours than you can imagine on the back of a horse, surveying our property. Don't worry, that pretty little top is safe with me. Safe as a jail cell. I won't let you get wet."

Just when she smiled at him, just when it looked like everything between them was going to get smoothed over, the heavens opened up and a steady stream of water came splashing down on them. In a split second, they were soaked.

Hannah slapped him on the shoulder. "Now, this just beats all," she exclaimed as Veronica stood up, squealed and trotted to her car.

As they stood there, watching Veronica get in the car, Hannah shook her head. "She's not the girl for you, Jarred. One day, you're going to realize that."

"And in the meantime?"

"In the meantime we might as well go get dry."

When Hannah turned and went inside the ice-cream shack, Jarred walked on back to his truck.

That moment, just as a blaze of lightning ignited the sky, a memory flashed of him and Serena the other night…their two bodies brushing against each other.

Of how sweet she'd tasted when he'd pressed his lips to hers. "Umbrellas, I'm finding, can be a heck of a good thing," he murmured.

After another few minutes, he'd unlocked the truck and got into the cab. Water dripped from his T-shirt and jeans, soaking the upholstery and making him chilled.

Lord, but he was a mixed-up idiot. The other night,

he'd been entertaining all kinds of thoughts about Serena Higgens.

Now he'd good and messed up things with Veronica. Shoot. It would serve him right if she up and got pneumonia and was too sick to go to the auction.

He sneezed. And sneezed again. Maybe he was getting sick, too.

After driving home and showering, Jarred walked into his room to find Virginia waiting for him on his bed. "'Bout time you got out," she chirped as she jumped up and down, messing up his already messed-up sheets.

He tightened the towel around his waist. "Ginny, you shouldn't be hanging out in my room without letting me know. And stop jumping on my bed."

After two more jumps, she stopped. "But I had to talk to you."

"Get down, and then we'll talk."

Mulishly, she climbed off then slowly stopped in front of him. He tightened the towel around his waist. "Can this wait until I get dressed?"

"Uh-uh. Jarred, I've had a real bad day."

He fought the urge to smile. For Ginny, a bad day could mean anything from no peanut butter for lunch to a bee sting. Still holding his towel tight—ever thankful that Gwen had bought them all extra-large bath sheets—he sat gingerly beside her. "All right. Let's hear it. Did you get in another fight?"

"Daddy was sick today."

All thoughts of bee stings flew out the window. "What? Did Daddy say he wasn't feeling well?"

She nodded, her bottom lip in a pout. "It's true. Daddy said he wasn't feeling too good, so he couldn't take me riding like he said he would."

"I bet he was just tired."

"Maybe, but I think the doctor at the hospital said his heart was sick. Daddy now has to stay home in bed and rest."

In the span of two seconds, Jarred felt his whole world come crashing down. Suddenly, everything he thought was important turned on its side and faded to black. "Daddy...I mean Dad was in the hospital? Are you sure?"

"Oh, yes," she said earnestly, her bright blue eyes staring at him. "It was kinda scary and exciting, too. Gwen and Trent took him in. I stayed with Junior." Ever the reporter, she continued. "Trent was going to call you, but Daddy said for him to stop his worrying and relax."

A little bit of irritation started coursing through him. A bit of hard feelings, too. "Trent should have called. Junior should have, too." After all, he was the oldest. This family was his responsibility, too. His brothers should have known that.

"They said we were to leave you alone 'cause someone told Trent they'd seen you having ice cream with Miss Veronica. Trent and Junior said you looovvve Miss Veronica."

"Hannah was there, too. And I wasn't doing anything wrong, so don't make it sound like I was."

Her eyes widened as hurt filled them.

"Besides, other people don't mean nothing compared to family." Even though she was only five, he looked to Virginia for support. "You understand that, right?"

She nodded solemnly. "Uh-huh." Hopping off the bed, she did a little spin. "Um, things are better now anyway. They sent Daddy on home with a bunch of instructions. Now we're all going to concentrate on making him better." Brightening, she did a little hop. "Guess what? I drew him a picture."

"That will make him real happy, honey. I know it will. Now get on out of here while I put my clothes on. When I'm dressed, I'll go get some answers."

She sidled to the door. "Are you glad I came in here to tell you?"

"I'm real glad." He kissed her forehead. "Now get, 'cause I'm getting cold."

She opened the door. "Jarred, now that I told you all about Daddy, you won't tell him that I got in trouble today at school, will you?"

"So, you were fighting again?"

She looked down. "Maybe."

"With Billy?"

"Kind of."

"Virginia Riddell, what is it going to take for you to leave that poor boy alone?"

"He just ignores me otherwise."

"We'll talk later. I won't tell Dad if you get on out."

"We don't want to make him mad."

"You need to learn to act like a little lady."

"That's boring."

"It's important." With some dismay, he realized he was starting to sound an awful lot like Serena. What was up with that?

"One day, are you going to bring Miss Veronica over?"

"I don't know."

That nonanswer seemed to suffice. She turned away.

Grabbing a pair of boxers and jeans, he practically closed the door in her face. Yeah, he'd give his little sister some news…and then he was going to have plenty to say to his other two siblings. But he wasn't going to be near as nice or patient.

They should have called him. He was the oldest. He was used to making sure everything and everyone was taken care of.

There was no way things were going to change now. Not now. Not ever.

Chapter Nine

When he was dressed, he met Virginia standing outside his door. Unable to resist her look of worry, he decided to leave all conversations about fighting for later and held out a hand. "Let's go see how's he's doing."

"He's not good. I told you that," she exclaimed as they walked down the hall and up the stairs to his father's suite. He was just about to push the door open when Gwen came out, her expression serious.

He clutched her elbow. "What's going on? How bad is he? And more important, why in the hell didn't y'all call me?" he said, his voice rising. "I can't believe I had to find out about Dad going to the hospital from Virginia."

Warily, Gwen looked toward Ginny, who was glancing from one to the other of them with a worried frown. "Keep your voice down," she warned.

"I will. When you give me some answers."

"Your dad's going to be okay. He had some chest pains for a bit but he seems to be doing better."

"When did all this happen? He was fine when I saw him this morning." He tried to recall exactly how his father looked at breakfast, but couldn't remember anything out of the ordinary.

"Don't panic. It all just happened a few hours ago. His arm started going numb and he said his chest hurt. Right away, he knew he needed help. Luckily, Trent was with him, so he ran him down to First General."

As Jarred visualized the scene, he felt sick. Never in his life had he ever heard his father back out of anything. Never saw him weak.

Never saw him as anything other than the strongest man in the room. "You're making this whole episode sound way too normal. This isn't. Dad doesn't get sick."

Stealing another look at Virginia, Gwen's voice hardened. "I'm telling you again, Jarred. You need to calm down."

He knew what she meant. Gently placing a hand on his little sister's curls, he nodded. "I'm fine now. I promise. What happened?"

"They ran a few tests and found out that he didn't actually have a heart attack, but that all the signs are there. After they finished at the hospital, the doctors there called Doc. He stopped by when your dad got back."

What the heck? "So, Dad's been in the emergency room, getting seen by Doc, and according to you, everything's hunky-dory. I can't believe nobody called me," he said again.

"*I* told you, Jarred," Virginia protested, clearly irritated. "I told you as soon as I could."

Feeling bad, he knelt down and clasped her pudgy hand. Squeezing gently, he said, "I know you did. You told me, and I'm grateful." The moment Ginny smiled, Jarred looked up toward Trent, who had just exited his father's room. "I meant, I can't believe you didn't call me when y'all were at First General. Earlier."

"Honestly, Jarred, stop being in such a snit about being informed. Things were crazy. Dad's blood pressure was through the roof."

"If it was so bad, don't you think he should still be in the hospital? You should've put your foot down, Trent, and told them what you thought about him getting shuffled around."

"You weren't there, so stop with the advice. Doc said we could watch him here just as well." A muscle in Trent's jaw was twitching something awful...obviously he was about to lose his patience. "That was the right decision. You know as well as I do what a stinker of a patient he would be. And like I said, Doc told us he could be watched at home."

"Sorry. I guess you're right."

"Guess?"

"I know you were right. Happy?"

Now that he'd finally been listened to, Trent held out a packet of papers. "Here's what the doctor suggested. You might want to skim over it for a few minutes."

"I will."

Trent gestured to the door. "Dad's been asking about you. When you're ready, you can go on in."

While Gwen walked off with Trent and Virginia, Jarred took a few moments to read the doctor's report. Much of it he didn't understand, though the phrases "high blood pressure" and "in danger of heart attack" jumped out at him.

After schooling his emotions as best he could, Jarred knew he couldn't wait another moment. Pushing back his father's door, he entered the dim room. Instantly, he was enveloped with the comforting, familiar smells of the past. A lingering scent of leather and Chaps cologne permeated everything.

As quietly as he could, he padded across the thick charcoal-gray carpet, ready to sit by his father's bedside and keep watch.

"If you're looking for a body, you won't find one there," his father called out from across the room. "I'm over here, son. On the couch."

Quickly Jarred changed directions, stumbling a bit when

he noticed his father's pallor reflecting in the soft glow of his reading light.

Wrapped in a thick hunter-green robe, his dad looked almost small—quite a feat for a 230-pound man. In front of him was a glass of water and the remains of a bowl of chicken noodle soup.

Two magazines were strewn in front of him, his reading glasses lying on top.

But it didn't look as if his dad had been doing much of anything beyond sitting in the dim light.

Something definitely was off. "You should be in bed."

"Not while it's daylight, I shouldn't. Stop lurking, boy, and come over here and have a seat."

Jarred bypassed the spot on the couch next to him and took the easy chair instead. That way he'd be able to look his dad over without being too obvious about it. "I heard you've had quite a day."

"Ain't no big thing. My blood pressure's acting up again."

"I didn't know it was ever acting up at all. You should have told me, Dad."

"I didn't want to worry you."

"Now I'm going to worry about you all the time."

His father rolled his eyes. "Lucky me."

"Dad, I would have tried to help you."

"Maybe that's why I didn't say a word. I'm old but not helpless. I didn't think I needed help."

"From what these papers say, it looks like Doc Johnson thought otherwise. And that he's thought you needed help for some time. Would've been nice if you had shared that with us."

His father looked away. "Maybe you're right. I guess my body has decided to show its age from time to time."

"With better food and the right medicine, it sounds like

things can get back on track. We don't need another episode like today."

"I'm with you. My trip to the hospital scared your little sister to no end. Disappointed her, too. She was counting on a pony ride today."

Since Virginia probably needed a talking-to about her behavior, Jarred thought it was likely a good thing she got no pony ride. "I'll deal with her later."

"Thanks. It won't do to forget about things like that. She's just a little thing." He slumped against the couch, showing every bit of his sixty-two years. "So. Ginny told me you've developed a fondness for Veronica Snow."

"Virginia talks too much. Probably can't count on much of what she says, you know."

"I wouldn't tell her that. She's just like her mother in that way—sure that every word she utters is the only way to go. She'd give you what-for before you knew which end was up."

"Perhaps."

"Veronica is quite a pretty thing."

"She is, at that."

His father's eyes turned wistful. "I knew her mother once upon a time."

"I didn't know that."

"It was back in high school."

"Did y'all date?"

"For a time. I took her to a dance or two. Then I met your mother and I couldn't think of another girl."

To hear his mother referred to as a girl made Jarred smile. "I guess not. Mom was special."

"Oh, yes, she was." His father's expression went soft and far away…just like it always did whenever they talked about June Riddell. "Your mother was special. She was a real lady."

Jarred's memories of his mother involved her whipping her

three boys into shape…but making cookies, too. Of riding her paint slow and easy on Saturday mornings, and dressing up for church on Sundays.

She'd been a good woman. Pretty. Happy with herself and with her life. And with them.

Pretty darned near perfect.

That's what he aimed to have for himself one day. A woman like that. A woman to make his family proud. "I think Veronica is a real lady, too."

"Perhaps. Though, I found out the hard way that sometimes it's real difficult to know what a woman's really like."

Jarred knew that to be true. Women were hard to trust. But what could he do? He needed somebody. And Ginny did, too.

After a moment, his dad raised a brow. "Your talkative sister told me you've decided to take up charm school. That true?"

"No, sir." When one of his father's eyes narrowed, Jarred amended his words. "I mean, I don't know. Serena Higgens is giving me a few pointers on being a gentleman. Ladies like Veronica need someone a little less rough around the edges, I think."

"A *Riddell* gentleman?" Cal Sr. gave a bark of laughter. "I didn't know that was possible."

"Mom always thought it was," Jarred said in defense.

"She did…but Carolyn thought differently."

The same sick feeling that always engulfed him when he heard Carolyn's name flooded back. "Carolyn was all wrong for us, Dad."

"She was. I've never been so happy to see someone walk out of my life." After a pause, his dad spoke again. "You know, I always thought you might fall in love with someone a little more down-to-earth, but you may be right about looking for a lady. Ever since we found oil, I've been hoping to give you boys a better life. To launch you into society. Better manners might help."

"They can't hurt."

"If you marry a city girl like Veronica, your children might think about going to college instead of the rodeo circuit. There's something to be said about yearning for a life that doesn't involve sitting on the back of a bull for eight seconds."

Hearing his father put down his many accomplishments made Jarred sad. "What you did in the ring was special, Dad. We knew it and Mom knew it, too. We've always been proud of you. Always."

"I'm grateful for that. But when we bought this house and Junior started community college, I started thinking that maybe we could get a little bit of class."

"I'm working on it."

"Well, tell me all about these lessons. Do you think you can learn something from Serena?"

"I think so. She's a regular encyclopedia of proper behavior."

"You listening to her?"

"Sometimes. Sometimes not." Thinking about all his mistakes, Jarred shared the story about nearly dropping Serena when he was pretending to help her from the car. "Thank goodness Serena has quick reflexes."

As Jarred had hoped, his father laughed. "And the patience of a saint! What else has Serena been teaching you?"

"The other day, she tried to teach me about carrying an umbrella for a woman, but it was a wash."

"It sounds easy enough."

"Well, it was a complete waste of time. I almost poked her eye out, and then today when it was raining, Veronica still got soaked to the skin."

"Funny thing about umbrellas," his father mused. "Unless one's over your head, you still get wet."

"That's a good point."

"Well, no matter what, I have to say that spending time with Serena is probably a good thing."

His father's comment took him by surprise. Serena was bossy and unappreciative of his efforts. "Why's that?"

"I was good friends with her dad. I always felt bad for her, having to live with the knowledge that her dad got hurt the way he did. In spite of everything, she's got a good head on her shoulders."

"She does have a good head on her shoulders, but we're just friends. That's all," he said rather testily. "Fact is, Serena's in a bit of financial trouble. I'm just trying to help her out some."

"That's good of you. She needs you, Jarred."

He blinked. "Needs me?"

"Sure. She's always been good to you. She's a girl you can trust. And she needs to trust you, too…" With a yawn, his father's eyes fluttered shut. "I think that doctor gave me a bit too much to think about today. I'm going to take a little nap." One eye opened. "Don't tell nobody, now."

"No, sir. You're on the couch. No one will think you're sleeping." He was going to say more, but his father's eyes were already shut.

As quietly as he could, he stood and padded out.

Virginia was there waiting. Before she could get a chance to worry, Jarred slipped an arm around her shoulders. "It's all done raining. What do you say we go have our talk now?"

"I'd rather go riding."

"Me, too. But someone's got to talk to you about hitting poor Billy. It might as well be me."

Walking as if she was going to the gallows, she shuffled

her steps. "I'm gonna be nicer. One of these days," she grumbled.

He placed a hand on her shoulder. "One of these days needs to come pretty soon, don'tcha think?" But as they walked down the hall, he felt his mind drift.

Back to his father's doctor's report. And his mom.

Of rain and umbrellas and being a little boy.

And thinking that his father was invincible.

Though that time was just yesterday, he was already missing that feeling something fierce.

Chapter Ten

"Serena, you hear about Calvin Riddell?" Hannah asked. "I just was on the phone with my daughter. Cal was in the hospital."

"Are you sure?"

"Positive. Bella said he almost had a heart attack yesterday."

"That's horrible." Concern for the patriarch of the Riddell family hit her hard. Cal Sr. had never been one for libraries, but he'd always had a kind word for her. She sure hoped he was going to be okay. "Well, what happened? Where are they?"

"I don't know too many details other than they're home now."

Immediately, Serena felt better. Home wasn't the hospital, which meant Cal Sr.'s episode hadn't been life threatening. Hoping to get her composure again, she exhaled. "Well, thanks so much for letting me know. We'll send a get-well card to his house."

Hannah nodded. "Cal Sr. is a tough old bird, but he's a sweetie, too. I sure wouldn't want anything to happen to him."

Her voice turned dreamy as she continued. "I've known him for years. His wife was darling."

"I remember her some. She was a good woman."

Hannah looked out the window at the parking lot. "I might

see if I can bring a casserole by. Gwen cooks some, and Jarred does, too, but they might appreciate it."

Thinking about casseroles made her think of Jarred looking at those cookbooks. "I'll give them a call, too." Serena wondered how Jarred was doing. She knew he loved his father dearly, in spite of the older man's notorious crankiness.

"I think you should, dear," Hannah murmured before walking over to a couple who needed help at a computer terminal.

Just as Veronica Snow flew in through the door. As usual, she was dressed to kill. Today, she wore a beautiful strapless silk sundress and fancy red high-heeled sandals.

But what was really catching Serena's eye was the look of determination on Veronica's face. She was a woman on a mission.

When she practically skidded to a stop in front of the reception counter, Serena smiled a welcome. "Hi, Veronica. May I help you?"

"Maybe. Actually, I'm hoping for some advice."

Serena was glad she'd had practice covering up her emotions. At the moment, she couldn't have been more surprised. Veronica Snow was the most put-together woman she'd ever met. Serena couldn't imagine what she could offer the socialite. "I'll be glad to help you if I can."

"I was hoping you'd say that." Picking up a worn copy of an Agatha Christie mystery, Veronica scanned the back of it before looking at Serena again. "Serena, people say you and Jarred Riddell are real good friends."

"We have known each other for ages," she allowed.

"Well, I hope this doesn't sound conceited, but I think he likes me. Really likes me."

Though the words were hard to hear, Serena forced herself to be supportive. "I know he does."

"He's not really my type. But now that I'm here, I mean stuck here in Electra for some time, I'm thinking maybe I should give him a chance. After all, he is very well-off. And attractive." She bit her lip. "In his own way."

Funny how all of a sudden Serena felt so protective of Jarred. He was much more than Veronica was saying. Much more than she probably had ever imagined. But if she said too much, all she'd get for it was a big wad of embarrassment. "He is all that," she said just as Hannah came back their way and joined in.

"He's a good man," Hannah said. "And handsome."

"Jarred is really good-looking. And all his attention and smiles have grown on me. At first he drove me crazy, but now it's kind of cute."

Hannah chuckled. "Now isn't that something. You two might be starting something special and you don't even know it!"

"So, anyway. Since you know him well and all…I just wanted to make sure he was, you know…a decent sort of person, right?"

"He is." Her answer felt choked out of her, especially since she'd spent most of her life doing her best not to even think about Jarred Riddell in any way other than as a good friend.

"And there's not anything between the two of you, is there?"

"Not at all. We're just friends."

"I heard he's been hanging out around here lately…"

"He's been doing that forever," Serena lied. "He's a big reader."

"So if we did date, you wouldn't care?"

For an instant, a knot of jealousy, tight and hard, settled in her stomach. Both Veronica and Jarred were getting everything she'd always wanted—a partner. A person who really appreciated them.

Unfortunately, neither seemed to understand how special that was.

But their love life was none of her business.

At the moment, manners were, and she needed to remember that. "I think if y'all started dating, it would make Jarred really happy."

"Thanks for talking to me about this." A winsome smile lit her face. "I guess I just didn't want to make a mistake or anything."

"Of course not."

She stepped backward. "Well, I better get going. I hate to leave my mom alone for too long."

"She's still having a time of it?" Hannah asked.

Veronica nodded.

"Let us know if we can help in any way," Hannah said kindly.

"I will," Veronica replied. "Thanks so much. Thanks for the advice, and for listening to me, too." Two lines formed on her forehead that only served to make her look even prettier, more approachable. "I don't have a lot of friends here. I really do appreciate your kindness."

"It's nothing. Don't worry, now." Serena gave a smile and a little wave before watching her new friend leave—and felt like three times the heel.

Oh, what a fake she was! Here she was, supposedly doing her best to get Jarred and Veronica together, but most times, all she felt was jealous.

Remembering what one of the authors in the charm-school books she'd been reading had said, about how women shouldn't divulge *all* their secrets, Serena felt her cheeks heat.

After all, she had a very good feeling that if her secrets were known, why, she'd be going straight to hell.

"CAN YOU MAKE MY EGGS over easy?" Junior called out to Jarred from the kitchen table.

"Only if you want those over-easy eggs scrambled," Jarred replied as he poured the rest of his egg batter into the pan. After sitting with the rest of his family near his father's bedside for most of the evening, he'd volunteered to make a simple meal of eggs, biscuits and bacon.

His brother, of course, didn't know how to accept a good thing and seemed to be doing his best to rile him up. "What about gravy? It's hardly right to have biscuits without gravy to go on top. Are you making any?"

"Nope."

"What kind of meal is this, anyway?"

"The only kind you're getting."

"Fine."

Jarred would have slugged Junior for being such a twit, but he noticed a slump to his younger brother's shoulders and a definite lack of pepper in his tone.

Actually, Junior sounded fairly deflated.

Kind of how he felt. "Go sit down. Food's almost ready."

"'Bout time."

"Oh, leave him alone, Junior," Trent said. "Me and Ginny are just glad he's cooking, aren't we, honey?"

Ginny nodded solemnly…just as a tear traipsed down her face. "I've got a sad. I'm worried about Daddy."

As Trent scooped up their baby sister and pulled out a handkerchief—*a handkerchief?*—to wipe her tears, and Junior murmured all kinds of sweet things, Jarred hung his head.

He was worried, too.

Truth was, the last visit with the doctor hadn't been too good. Their father needed surgery, but it would be a risky one, thanks to his lifelong habit of smoking cigars and the fact that he was holding on to about fifty extra pounds.

Calvin Barrett Riddell Sr. had always been invincible. Hardworking, optimistic, and raising his three boys with an iron will. He'd watched over them like a hawk in high school. There had never been a kegger that he hadn't known about or a date he hadn't seen coming.

Even when the days were so dark after their mother died, Cal Sr. had stayed strong for their sakes.

But during the past twenty-four hours, he'd seemed a shadow of his former self.

Weak. So, so weak.

It was troublesome.

Carefully spooning the eggs onto an oval platter, Jarred added bacon and carried it out to the table. Then he pulled the full tray of carefully cut biscuits into a basket and made sure there was strawberry jam on the table, too.

"Jarred, you made circle biscuits!" Ginny exclaimed.

"Just for you, sugar," he said with a smile. Until Ginny had made her preferences known, they'd always been a drop-biscuit kind of family.

His brothers didn't say much, but Jarred felt the deep sense of satisfaction that came from watching his siblings dig into his simple meal, even if it was breakfast for dinner.

Once again, he was glad he'd learned to cook at least a few things real well. He enjoyed the challenge of making something tasty out of a few simple ingredients. In addition, it gave him something to do during difficult times like this. Sitting around and worrying would have driven him to drink.

'Course, times were so tough, he figured he could probably manage to drink and cook at the same time.

He'd just cleaned his plate when the doorbell rang.

"I'll get it," Ginny said, sliding off her chair.

"And I'll help you," Trent called out to her, just as she

scampered out of sight. "Virginia, don't you open the door without me there."

Jarred traded a glance with Junior. "Trent's good with her. Patient."

"We're all good with that little rabbit. Well, until she needs to be disciplined. Then, I'm pretty much no good."

Thinking of Ginny's penchant for fighting, Cal grinned. "That's why she has Dad."

"Dad's good with her, though not hardly tough enough."

Maybe it was his dad's surgery or maybe it was just seeing Ginny's smile, but for a moment Jarred turned nostalgic. "Dad was over the moon when he found out Carolyn was having a girl. Remember the way he went out and bought all that pink and lace?"

"He practically bought out the store," Trent said with a smile.

Jarred was about to bring up the moment they'd all spied Ginny's ten tiny toes and fallen in love—when he heard the unmistakable voice of Serena Higgens floating down the hall.

What in the heck was she doing there? He stood abruptly and went to the front hall.

Trent had just leaned in and kissed her cheek. "Serena, it's good to see you," he drawled. "You're lookin' good."

"I look all right. Nothing like a rodeo star. You're doing us all real proud, Trent."

To Jarred's dismay, his youngest brother blushed. "I've gotten lucky, that's all."

"It takes more than luck to show a bull who's boss." She turned to Jarred. "Don't you think?"

"Maybe." Unable to stand the suspense, he said, "Why are you here?"

"Oh. Well, Hannah told me about your dad. I came over to see if y'all needed anything."

"We're good. You didn't need to go to no trouble."

Trent winked. "But I'm glad you did. Come on in and take a load off."

Serena stepped forward and took Trent's proffered arm, as if they were center stage at a debutant ball. As they walked away, Jarred watched them for a moment.

And wondered why he had an insane urge to pull the two of them apart. Surely she hadn't ever had feelings for Trent... had she?

'Cause she should know that he was nothing but a good-time guy. He was never going to stick around for anyone. Ever.

"They look real cute together," Junior sassed, coming up beside him.

"You know Serena. She's just friends with all of us. That's it."

A slow, sly smile lit his brother's face. "No, she's been your buddy. The rest of us just looked at her and pined."

"What are you talking about?"

"I think you know."

He didn't. But he didn't want to make a big deal out of it, neither.

If Jarred moved slightly to the side, he could just see Trent's left shoulder as he gestured at something out the window. Trent's shoulder and a good portion of Serena's backside. And her swath of long hair.

"You going out to join them?"

"Hell, yeah." But as he walked through the kitchen to get his hat, he spied a whole mess of dishes still waiting to be cleaned up. The remains left on them getting harder to scrub off by the second.

From the other room, he heard Trent tease Serena, and she laughed. He heard Virginia call out for Junior to play ball outside.

Either he could corral the lot of them into the kitchen or he could roll up his sleeves and do the work himself.

There was really only one choice. With a sigh, he turned the water on hot and pulled out the dish soap.

Chapter Eleven

"Jarred, why don't we postpone our next meeting?" Serena said into the receiver the moment he picked up her call. "You've got a lot going on."

"Oh, not so much. We have a meeting planned, and I want to honor that. I don't want to cancel on you, Serena."

For a moment, she almost smiled. Jarred probably didn't realize it, but he was being incredibly gentlemanly toward her. Without skipping a beat he was putting her needs in front of his. It was very thoughtful. And, to her way of thinking, a difficult thing for most men to do.

Perhaps all her lessons were making a difference.

But what also struck her was the tone in his voice. His usual lazy twang sounded stretched impossibly thin. He was worn-out and stressed…and she didn't want to add to it.

"Listen, I know your dad's feeling poorly. And you've got a lot of responsibilities. I noticed that when I stopped by."

"I still can't believe you did stop by."

"You sound upset. Are you?"

"Of course not."

"All right, then, so I guess you understand why I don't want to interfere."

"Me going about my day won't make him any worse. Shoot, chances are, if I just sit in his room staring at him some more, he's going to get even more irritable."

"More irritable? Has your dad been grumpy?"

"As a bear."

Serena gripped her receiver hard. Boy, did she wish she was sitting across from him instead of on the phone. All his usual sayings sounded flat and depressed.

He sounded as though he could really use a friend. She tried to think if he looked different at all when she'd stopped by their house. But he hadn't been around all that much.

Actually, he'd been in the kitchen most of the time, doing dishes. "How…how is your father doing, health-wise?"

"Better. Well, as good as a guy who almost had a heart attack can be."

"I really am sorry about everything."

"Me, too." He sighed. "I wish he was a better patient, though. At the moment, nothing's making him happy. Right now, we're trying to convince Dad to take it easy. He's supposed to nap and relax. Watch television. Read books."

"Those sound like good things."

"They are, but I don't think he knows how to do any of that. He's always been a list-making type A guy. Lolling around the house don't come naturally."

"I'm sorry." And she was. So sorry that she didn't even bother trying to fix his grammar.

"I'm sorry, too." A hint of wistfulness colored his tone before he cleared his throat. "See, that's why as far as our lesson goes, I don't think postponing it would be a good idea. We've got a lot to cover. We both know I'm almost a lost cause."

"You're not a lost cause."

"I'm pretty darn close. At least, I feel that way."

Serena didn't know if she was more surprised about him admitting that he was willing to be helped, or that he was still so determined to do the auction.

All of a sudden, she worried that she'd been too hard on

him. That she'd made him think that he wasn't worthy of some snooty society girl. "Jarred, you know…there's nothing wrong with you the way you are. In the ways that count, you're pretty perfect."

"The hell you say."

Her grip relaxed. Now she could almost see him smiling. "No, I mean it. Most women would be thrilled to do anything with you. I bet you'll get a high bid at the auction even if Veronica doesn't bid on you."

He tapped the phone. "Are you sure this is Serena Higgens? The Serena I know isn't near so kind to me. The Serena I know never misses an opportunity to put me in my place."

"I haven't been that bad."

"You ain't been that good."

"Don't say *ain't.*"

"See? You never stop." His voice turned warm. "Never."

She almost chuckled, knowing that he'd inserted that little *ain't* just to get her going. Of course, her correcting him was for the same purpose. By now their give-and-take felt special and fun. As if it was something only the two of them could ever share.

That made her think again about the reason for her call. "Now, stop joking for a second and listen to me. I'm trying to be serious!"

"I know. I'm surprised, that's all."

"Well, you shouldn't be. We might have had our differences from time to time, but I still think you're going to be a great success."

"I just don't want to be embarrassed."

"Believe me, I'm sure you won't be embarrassed. You're gonna be just fine." Actually, she was sure he was going to be better than that.

And it was also too funny how Jarred was talking. Almost as though he thought he was the only person on earth to have ever feared public humiliation. From her own experiences, she knew he wasn't.

"How can you be so sure of that? Are you going to bid?"

"I wish I could. But you know I don't have any money for that."

"I'm just teasing. I wouldn't expect you to want me anyhow."

She would. "You might be surprised."

"You're joshing me again! Don't turn chicken on me now, Serena. You've done nothing but fuss about the way I talk, eat, carry umbrellas and chew."

Images flashed of their time together. Images of them eating ice cream and chatting. And getting uncomfortably close under umbrellas.

And then the irony hit her. Here she was, doing her all-fire best to make him into someone bright and new…and she was still completely infatuated with the man he'd always been.

But that didn't help his situation. "Perhaps you could get Veronica another way?"

"Even if I decided to do that, it won't matter. I promised the city council that I'd participate in the auction. I don't have a choice. I made a promise."

"Yes, I guess you did." And he wasn't the type of man to back out of a promise.

"Yep. I need the help and the auction is just around the corner. We have no time to lose."

"But surely other things are more important than…" Her voice drifted off. How could she put into words what she was thinking without offending his goal or Veronica? "Than auctions?"

"It's a commitment. And a promise. Listen, Serena, I think things are going better anyway. Just the other day, I passed her at the coffee shop, and she went so far as to say hello."

She laughed. "That's progress."

"In no time at all, she might even shake my hand."

From the safety of her bedroom, Serena grinned. Oh, but he made her smile. He always had.

"Hey, how about you come over here for a lesson? That way I can still check on my dad."

"I can do that, if you're sure."

"I'm sure. This auction involves table manners, Serena. There's no telling what I'm doing wrong."

"Don't worry. I bet you're doing everything wrong," she teased. Well, only half teased.

"Great. Eight o'clock?"

"I'll be there," she said before hanging up.

Then she looked around and wondered what had gotten into her. She was actually looking forward to seeing him.

Looking forward to his smile and the way he made her feel as though she was the only person who really understood him. As though she was someone special in his life who really mattered.

Well, when he wasn't mooning over Veronica.

She couldn't help it; she smiled. Suddenly, the thought of Jarred picking up the wrong fork or blowing his nose during a meal didn't sound all that scandalous. It sounded like Jarred.

Which was the completely wrong thing to think. The two of them had lived in the same town practically all their lives. She'd sat behind him in Geometry and he'd teased her in a good-natured, *friendly* way.

Now he was using her to get the attention of someone prettier and more successful. She was his means to an end. She needed to remember that.

When the phone rang again, she picked it up quickly. "Jarred, what else did you forget?"

"Um, Serena? I mean, Miss Higgens? This isn't Jarred. It's actually Pete Ross. From the bank."

"Hey, Pete," she replied. "What's going on? And what's with the Miss Higgens and telling me you're from the bank? We've known each other for ages."

"I'm, uh, on an official call right now."

"Oh?"

"Serena, the fact is, you're overdrawn."

"Oh, my goodness!" As the words echoed in her ear, she winced. It probably wasn't possible to sound any more like a silly fool. But as reality set in, the nervous pit in her stomach expanded to the size of a watermelon. "By how much?"

"Sixty dollars."

She swallowed. All things considered, it wasn't too much. But since she wasn't due to get paid for another eight days, it might as well be a thousand dollars. Thinking back to the last time she balanced her checkbook, she said, "I don't understand how that could have happened. I had almost a hundred in it on Saturday."

"I'm looking at the screen now, Serena. Maybe you had a couple of bills you forgot about?" He paused. "Here's an automatic withdrawal for insurance. Did you remember to deduct that?"

There surely couldn't be anything more demeaning than going through her bank account with Pete Ross as if she was in sixth grade.

But shoot, she had forgotten about that blasted insurance!

After a lengthy pause, he cleared his throat. "It's also my duty to tell you that you have a fine."

"A fine?"

"Yes. From me."

"You?"

"I mean, us. The bank. We had to charge you for writing a bad check. We covered for you but charged you thirty dollars."

"Is that part of the sixty I owe?"

"Oh, no. It's in addition. I am sorry to tell you the bad news."

He really did sound mortified. Poor guy. "I see. Thank you for calling, Pete. I'll see if I can borrow some money from my sister." Oh, she hated doing that. "I'll be in tomorrow with—"

"I could lend you some money if you want."

She nearly dropped the phone. "I'm sorry, Pete…but what did you say?"

"I, um, I don't want you to worry so much. I'd be happy to help you out."

"But, Pete, wouldn't that be a conflict of interest or something?"

"Not if it was a loan between friends." He chuckled. But it was forced. A little high-pitched sounding. "And we are that, right? I mean, we have known each other forever."

"Since grade school—"

"That's a long time." As he continued, his voice became a little bit more sure. "You know, Seri, we never did meet for coffee."

Serena couldn't figure out how he managed it, but his slow reminder set off a slew of warning bells, loud and shrill. "You're right. We never did. We'll have to do that sometime." She closed her eyes. Her promise sounded as weak as ever.

"Since we have a date set in the future, why don't you let me help you?"

He sounded so sincere. Plus, well…she really had no choice. She was in dire financial straights. Beggars and choosers and all that. "All right," she said, wishing the moment she said the words that she could take them right back. "But only a hundred dollars. And I promise to pay you back as soon as I get my paycheck."

"Don't you worry about that right now."

She frowned. "I'll be worrying."

"I hope not for long. Now that we have that settled, please say yes to letting me take you out to dinner. Tonight."

Little pinpricks of doubt began dotting her skin. "Actually, Pete, I don't feel much like eating."

"You must. After all, we have something to celebrate."

They did? Now she was getting seriously creeped out. In all the years she'd known him, they'd never done more than talk casually at community events. Did he now think she owed him something? "Pete, you know I can't afford a dinner out."

"That's why I'm asking you. It's my treat."

"That's very kind of you, but I'm already borrowing money from you—"

"We both know one thing has nothing to do with the other."

But it kind of felt as if it did. Serena leaned back and wished she could throw the phone out the window. These latest conversations she was having were throwing her for a loop. "Well…"

"Say yes."

"Well, all right." She was being silly. Pete was so nice. And, well, a dinner out would be a treat. "It can't be a very long dinner. I've got a meeting at eight," she apologized. There was no way she could cancel on Jarred. He was paying her for her time.

Kind of how Pete was, too?

Her stomach cramped up some more.

"Then how about we eat early?" he asked smoothly. "At six-thirty? We could visit and catch up and I could give you that loan."

Oh, she didn't like how he was bringing up that loan already. "Six-thirty is just fine."

"I'll look forward to it."

She swallowed. What was going on with him? Usually the

somewhat nerdy Pete Ross was all buttoned up and circum-spect. But maybe he really was just looking forward to their dinner.

And, heck. Why was she overreacting, anyway? He was reliable and compassionate. And once more, he'd always been kind to her. Now he was even willing to give her a loan when she really needed it.

She should give him a chance. She knew she should. Good, stable guys were definitely not a dime a dozen. Maybe she would enjoy his company.

Besides, Jarred Riddell was simply a crush. One day he was going to hook that Veronica Snow and move on.

And he would. She would do well to not forget that.

Before things got stranger, she quickly replied. After all, she really didn't have a choice at all. She was overdrawn and she needed money. He was willing to help her. End of story. "Thank you, Pete. I'd love to meet you for dinner. That's so kind of you."

After a few more words about meeting him at the Golden Dove, she hung up, then looked longingly at her bed. If there had ever been a time when she wished she could crawl under the covers and hide from the world, this was it.

Her day couldn't be crazier. Never before had she had two meetings with two eligible bachelors.

Never before had she owed so much money to so many people.

Never before had she felt so out of control.

She hoped her heart could take it.

Chapter Twelve

"You look great, Serena," Pete said when she met him in the Golden Dove's ornately decorated bar. "That dress looks nice. Real nice."

"Thank you." Self-consciously, she smoothed down the royal-blue jersey knit that seemed to hug every curve. Tracy had given it to her for her birthday. After trying it on once, she'd stuck it in the back of her closet. In her opinion, it was too formfitting. She always felt as if every curve and bump was on display when she wore it…though, of course, Tracy had said that women's curves were a good thing.

For some reason, Tracy's comment had stuck in her mind that afternoon. So instead of her usual jeans and boots, she gathered her courage, pulled it out and slipped it on.

And to her surprise, the color did accent her hair well… and she had to admit that the royal-blue did make her green eyes a bit more vibrant.

Looking around at the beautiful hand-carved filigree surrounding the bar and the burgundy leather-covered bar stools, she said, "Eating here is such a nice treat. I've only dined here a few times."

"I don't go here often, either. But I thought, well, why not?" He smiled. "You only live once."

With some surprise, she noticed he had a dimple in his cheek. "That's exactly right."

"Wine?"

"Sure. That would be real nice. Thank you. Chardonnay?"

He signaled over the waiter. "Gin and tonic for me and a Chardonnay for the lady."

Serena eyed him a little longer. Here, out of the bank, he looked so confident. Better. When their drinks came, he lifted his to toast. "Here's to us, Serena."

Though the toast and the "us" connotation caught her off guard, his earnest expression made her shake off her lingering doubts. So did the fact that they were called to the table at that very moment.

As soon as they sat, Serena opened her menu and concentrated on her dinner choices. Perhaps if they ordered quickly, dinner would be over soon. She ended up picking shrimp and a salad because it didn't cost too much.

Pete ordered prime rib and another gin and tonic.

When they were alone again, he pulled out a white envelope and slid it across the red tablecloth to her. It stood out bright and blinding, like some mismatched valentine. "Here you go. I didn't want you to have to wait another moment for this."

Her cheeks flamed as the table of four watched her pick it up, then not so discreetly slip it in her purse. "Thank you." Needing to say something else, she said sincerely, "And thank you for calling me today to let me know about my bank account. I really do appreciate it."

"I'm glad I was able to save you from all that embarrassment." Looking her over, he said, "Besides, if helping you out is the best way to get you to go out with me, then I think I came up the winner. You know, I've been wanting to take you out for some time."

This was the second time he'd made that reference. "I'm sorry if I've forgotten, but I honestly don't remember you asking me out before. Ever."

"I have. Well, I've tried to gather up my courage," he said. "Remember six months ago when we knocked into each other at the grocery?"

She'd always felt that their "knock" hadn't been completely an accident. "Now I do. You, um, invited me over for steaks." There'd been two "butcher's specials" in Pete's basket. She'd looked at the meat that had already started to turn and ran away as fast as she could.

"Yep. I was going to ask you to be my date last year, too. To the banker's ball, but then I'd heard you weren't going to be in town."

"Well, here we are together. And it has nothing to do with the money." She really hoped she meant it. "I'm glad we finally were able to make this work."

"I'm really glad to hear that. Really glad."

She sipped her wine and tried to view his earnestness in a new light. It was flattering, right? "I'm glad that you're glad."

Luckily, their meals came and she concentrated on eating. Fast.

But Pete wasn't in such a hurry. Instead of picking up his fork, he stared hard at her. "Serena, I don't know if you knew, but I'm certified in scuba diving."

Huh? Where had this come from? And where was it going? "I didn't know that."

"Oh, yes. I've dived off the coast of several islands and plan to go again in just a few months. Did you know the reefs surrounding St. Thomas are supposed to be incredible?"

"No."

If he was disappointed with her less-than-enthusiastic response, he gave no indication. "It's true. Do you swim?"

"Some." Not that there were too many opportunities to swim anywhere in Electra. The community had never wanted to put much money into a recreation center—there were too many other needs around town.

He winked. "Maybe you'll consider driving over to Bardstown and joining the Y. You can take scuba lessons there. You never know when they'll come in handy. Who knows? Maybe one day someone tall, dark and handsome will invite you to go on a cruise to the Caribbean."

Slowly, she sipped her wine, wishing the glass had been a little bit more full. This was surely the most worrisome conversation she'd had in some time—and she'd thought Jarred's proposal of charm-school lessons would top just about anything.

"I'll think about that."

"Yes. Please do," he said, cutting off his first bite-size portion of meat.

Serena looked at the remains of her shrimp and salad with a sinking feeling. Usually she would have really enjoyed the chance to have a meal out. Especially at a nice restaurant like the Golden Dove.

But though she'd been wishing that some kind of spark would materialize, she now realized she could never think of him in a romantic way. Yes, she was really stuck between a rock and a hard place. She'd said yes to his loan and yes to his dinner because she wanted to be his friend. If their positions had been reversed, she knew she would have offered him assistance.

She was keeping her mouth shut during dinner because she felt she owed him.

But those realizations didn't make her feel any better about herself or her state of affairs.

Actually, fact was, he knew too much. He knew her bank account, he knew her financial troubles, and he wasn't afraid to use it all to his benefit. She felt like a caged animal at the zoo. Locked up and confined and forced to make the best of a bad situation.

After taking another bite, Pete grinned in obvious pleasure. "I do love a good steak, don't you?"

"Definitely." With a feeling of regret, she bit into a shrimp and chewed slowly.

And then almost choked when she saw Cal Jr. and Jarred walk through the front door and head their way. Oh, heaven help her. He still looked so good to her. So much better than Pete ever would.

Pete tapped his spoon on the table. "Serena, did you hear me? I just asked if you've ever spent much time at the honky-tonk. Billy Bob's. Have you?"

"Huh? Oh, no. I haven't."

"Maybe we should think about checking that place out sometime. I know it's a little out of the ordinary, but it might be fun."

"Well, I don't know about that, Pete. I don't know if bars are really my thing…."

"It might be fun."

"Maybe," she said noncommittally again. She couldn't help but let her eyes drift back to Jarred.

And wondered what he was thinking.

Chapter Thirteen

"This is the last time we're picking up food together for Dad, Junior," Jarred said as they wandered through the maze of fancy tables at the Golden Dove on their way toward the kitchen. "I feel like a wallflower, being seen here with you."

"Oh, get over yourself. The food here is awesome. Plus, it's not every day that we get an invitation to pay a visit to the Golden Dove's kitchens."

"You're such a foodie."

"This is a first-class place. Shoot. You were just as impressed as I was that it was highlighted by the Food Network last month."

Jarred did have to give him that. "It was pretty cool. Jean Claude looked great on TV."

As soon as Jean Claude Valentine, owner and chef of the nicest restaurant in the county, had heard about Cal Sr.'s illness, he'd volunteered to make a few low-fat and nutritious meals for him. Some might have thought it odd that such a famous guy would make such an offer, but to the two of them, it wasn't odd at all.

Over the years, the two men had formed an unlikely friendship. The slim, elegant proprietor had much in common with the rugged former rodeo rider. Both came from humble beginnings and both enjoyed hunting and fishing. That was plenty to build a friendship on, and it had lasted for over ten years.

"How about after we get Dad's meals, we head out to the Shack for burgers."

Junior nodded. "Sounds good. Even smelling all this food is making me hungry. Too bad we're not dressed right for this place. I'd pull out a chair right this minute."

Jarred glanced down at his jeans and boots. Sure enough, it was as he feared. Once again, he'd forgotten to change out of his work boots. The pair he was wearing were covered in mud and who knew what else. He was just about to check to see if he'd been tracking dirt in when he spied a shimmering curtain of silky black hair all dressed up in a blue dress. It looked suspiciously like Serena Higgens…but better. "Junior, hold up a sec."

Leaving his brother's side, Jarred strode around two waiters to get a better look. "Serena?"

When the gal's head popped up and revealed a pair of green eyes that he'd recognize anywhere, Jarred knew he'd hit pay dirt. "Hey. I didn't know you were eating dinner here tonight."

But instead of smiling in her usual way, she looked a little shifty. As if she was kind of embarrassed to be seeing him. "Hi."

He strode closer. When he noticed just how that clingy dress hugged her curves, he grinned. "Look at you! I don't know if I've ever seen you in a dress. You fill it out real good, sugar."

Serena ran her hands down her rib cage. "Um, thank you."

Because he'd never missed an opportunity that came his way, he watched her in true male appreciation. "I've never seen you wear that. I would have remembered. Is it new?"

"No. I mean, Tracy got it for me a while ago but I've never worn it out." Absently, she ran her fingers down the fold of fabric along her neckline.

But then, instead of smiling his way, she looked across the table. At…her date? Pete Ross?

Why?

About a hundred random things were going through his mind. How come he'd never noticed just how well-proportioned Serena was under her regular wardrobe of jeans and long, full skirts?

How come she was out with Pete? And how come he'd even asked her out? Last he'd heard, Pete didn't date. Ever.

Behind him, Junior came up. After he greeted Serena, he, too, looked at Pete. "Hey."

Serena exhaled, as if she was a part of something that couldn't be prevented. "I'm sure y'all know Pete Ross?"

"I do." Jarred shook Pete's hand. "Hey."

Pete stood up and smiled brightly. "Good to see y'all again. Hope you enjoy your dinner. You'll have to try the prime rib. The chef's outdone himself. It's really very good."

"It looks good," Junior said.

Still unable to stop looking at Serena, Jarred cut to the chase. "Actually, we're just picking up some meals for my dad. He's under the weather."

"I heard," Pete said. "I hope he's doing better."

"He is, well, I think he is. You know my dad. He's difficult on the best of days."

"We won't keep you, then."

There was something in Pete's eyes that gave Jarred a moment's pause. Or maybe it was something in Serena's expression. She looked kind of trapped. Kind of like a chicken with a fox in its coop.

Jarred felt ornery enough to take notice of it. He stuffed his hands in his back pockets and rocked back on the dirty heels of his boots. "You're not keeping us from too much. We're in no hurry."

Serena rolled her eyes.

And Pete, well, Pete glared. "We are. Our food is getting cold."

"Let's go. I've starving," Junior muttered. "See ya, Serena."

Jarred looked at Serena's plate. Her food looked half-gone and her knife and fork were crossed in the middle. "Serena's done." Showing off his newfound knowledge, he said, "She taught me all about silverware the other evening."

"Time to go," Junior said before adding a giant push on his spine.

They walked through the double doors into the kitchen just as Pete started talking again.

The moment they entered the kitchen Jean Claude greeted them with hugs and all worries about Serena were pushed to the side.

"Jarred! I'm so glad you stopped by," he said, every single one of his *s*'s sounding like *z*'s. "I have lots of food all ready to go."

"Thank you for helping us out. Dad's special diet was going to be beyond my skills in the kitchen."

"He should like these meals so much, he'll hardly notice that they're not full of fat and cholesterol."

Sharing a look with Junior, Jarred knew that was doubtful. Cal Sr. was a man who knew his sauces—and he'd never met a piece of red meat he didn't like.

"I hope you're right, Jean. Otherwise, we're going to have some trouble at home. He'll be hungry and grumpy and I'll have to deal with him."

"Then you'll be grumpy, too, eh?"

"I'm trying not to be." Pulling out his wallet, he looked around the kitchen. "Who should I pay?"

"I'm not going to charge you! It's my gift. As a friend."

"I know he'll appreciate that. Thank you." Rocking back on his heels, he realized he was directly in the path of several of Jean Claude's assistants. "We'll get out of your way now. I'm sure you've got lots to do."

Jean Claude picked up a bundle of broccoli. "There's always lots to do. That's a good sign. But first, you must eat, yes?"

Though Jarred could practically hear his brother salivating beside him, he pushed the temptation aside. They had food to deliver. And even he knew that their jeans and button-downs weren't fancy enough for the Golden Dove's dress code. "We couldn't do that to you."

"I insist. I have chicken and cod and some beautiful buffalo filets tonight. Say yes?"

"Hell, yes!" Junior answered before Jarred had time to open his mouth. "You know, when we walked in here, I felt like something the cat dragged in. But your offer is too good to refuse." He directed a you-better-know-what's-good-for-you look at Jarred. "Right?"

No way was he going to get between Junior and his food. "Right. Sure."

Next thing they knew, Jean Claude was ushering them back out to the dining room to the best table in the house—the one that faced the restaurant's kitchen.

Jean Claude kept that table empty for special guests. It was the only table where he served guests himself.

"We sure appreciate this," Jarred said.

"It's nothing." With a wave of his hand, he directed one of his waiters to bring them a menu before disappearing again into the kitchen.

"I can't believe we got so lucky!" Junior exclaimed. "What are you going to try?"

"Buffalo."

"Me, too. I don't know what that Pete was thinking. I'd never pass up bison for prime rib."

The mention of the banker's name led Jarred to glance over

Serena's way again. Though, who was he kidding? For some reason, he couldn't seem to stop staring at her.

But heck, she didn't look too good. Currently, she was twirling her empty glass between two hands and looking as if she'd just lost her best friend in the world.

After the server walked over and served them two glasses of sparkling water, Jarred leaned toward his brother. "What do you know about Serena and that banker?"

"Nothing."

"Really? But you're at the bank all the time."

"You know I deal with Mr. McKnight, the bank president."

"I wonder why Serena's hanging out with Pete? I don't think she does a whole lot of banking or investing. In fact, she told me she was in something of a financial mess. That's why she agreed to give me those lessons."

Junior grunted. "You're such an ass. Look at her. It's clear as day why Pete asked her out. She's beautiful."

Serena? Beautiful? He craned his neck and looked at her again. She did look pretty fetching.

After two bowls of piping-hot potato leek soup were delivered, Jarred did some thinking. Serena wasn't pretty in the way that Veronica was, but she certainly did have some good qualities. Those green eyes of hers reminded him of the gulf waters in the early morning. Her lips were a rosy soft color and shaped nice.

And that hair—so sleek and dark and fluid. It reminded him of crude oil just as it sprang from the ground. He couldn't even think about that figure of hers without remembering how perfect she'd felt in his arms.

In spite of himself, his gaze kept straying to her, wondering why she was out with Pete.

Just as Jean Claude brought out two plates of buffalo, Serena and Pete stood up to leave. Pete was grinning as if he'd won the lottery. Serena, on the other hand, looked as if she would rather be somewhere else.

Or…with anyone else? Then Pete rested his hand on her backside.

She flinched.

Pete, on the other hand, smiled some more.

"Ah, hell," Jarred muttered as he stood.

Jean Claude turned from his conversation with Junior. "What's wrong?"

"That damn banker is putting the moves on Serena. He just grabbed her ass." Jarred looked her way again and practically felt steam flow out of his ears as he watched Pete's hand hover over Serena's hip. "Oh, my Lord. He's doing it again." His fist clenched, already looking forward to making contact with Pete's face. "I'm going to kill him."

"He certainly has hands like spaghetti," Jean Claude observed.

"Pete's hands aren't your problem," Junior warned.

"Like hell they're not. Serena's my friend." Hardly aware of his brother's words of warning, he marched across the restaurant and belted the banker's jaw. With a groan, the idiot fell to the floor.

"Oh!" cried Serena.

"You ba…brat," Jarred said, keeping his language G-rated only for the sake of the other diners. "I can't believe you're manhandling librarians in broad daylight. Didn't your daddy ever teach you any manners?"

"Oh, for heaven's sakes, Jarred," Serena said. "Settle down. I'm fine."

"You wouldn't have been if I hadn't stepped in. I saw where he was placing his hands." Lowering his voice, he bent closer to her ear. "What's more, I saw how he was making you feel."

Serena flushed but said nothing.

Which made Jarred even more irritated when he stared down at Pete, who was moaning on the ground like an old woman. "Get up. I didn't hit you all that hard."

"I'm bleeding," Pete said, making no move to get to his feet. "I think you broke my nose."

"I should've broke your hand. I saw what you did. You're grabbing Serena's butt right here in the restaurant."

Nervous twitters surrounded them as Jarred realized his voice had risen.

Serena's face turned a darker shade of red. "Be quiet!"

Junior came up behind them. "Ma'am," he murmured to a passing diner before grabbing Jared's arm. "That was Edith Hanson. The preacher's wife. You're making a scene."

Jarred looked at Jean Claude, still holding the plate of buffalo. "Sorry, but I couldn't let her deal with that sucker alone."

Instead of looking horrified, Jean Claude only looked bemused. "So I see."

Finally getting to his feet, Pete stuffed a handkerchief to his nose. "You'll be hearing from my lawyer."

"Can't wait."

Pete reached out for Serena's arm. "Let's get out of here."

She jerked her arm away. "I don't think so." Next, she opened her pocketbook and handed an envelope to Pete. "I can't accept this."

"Serena, you're overdrawn."

Jarred wrapped an arm protectively around Serena's shoulders. "I'll help her out."

Pete brushed off his slacks before looking over the two of them derisively. "I just bet you will."

When he left the room, the whole restaurant seemed to breathe a sigh of relief.

Jarred was just complimenting himself on saving his

charm-school teacher when she turned on him, tears running down her cheeks. "This is why you need me. Gentlemen don't cause scenes in restaurants. You don't hit people. And most important, you stay out of things that aren't your business." With a hiccup, she cast a pleading look Jean Claude's way. "Mr. Valentine, I hate to ask you this, but could you please let me use your phone? I need to call a cab."

Junior stepped right in. "Don't even think about that. We'll take you home."

"I'll box up your food and bring it right out," Jean Claude said.

"Thank you. I really am sorry about all this," Junior said with a dark look Jarred's way.

But instead of looking shocked, the restaurateur merely looked amused. "No worries. I've been in far worse brawls."

"I'll wait for Dad's food. Take her outside, Jarred," Junior said.

As they walked out to the twilight, Jarred looked Serena's way. Now he was embarrassed. "I was just trying to help, you know."

For a moment, he didn't think she was going to answer. But then a sad little look appeared on her face. "I know."

"You didn't look happy to be with him. Were you?"

Her head hung. "I tried to be. But…no."

Reaching out, he linked his fingers through hers. "You going to stay mad at me for long?"

As twilight turned to night and the sky darkened to a black velvet, she slowly shook her head. "I might still be mad tomorrow."

He tugged her a little closer. "But the day after that?"

"I'll forgive you by then, I think."

"Fair enough," he murmured, pressing his lips to her knuckles, just as Junior came out carrying an oversize shopping bag.

Chapter Fourteen

The three of them climbed in Jarred's truck. Serena was in the middle, kind of wedged in close to him on account of Cal Jr.'s size and the giant bag of food.

Sitting so close to Jarred made it impossible for her to ignore all her stored-up, pushed-aside feelings for him. As usual, she couldn't care less that he wasn't all coiffed and fashionable. She liked him exactly as he was—all muscle and rough edges. She liked the feel of his denim-clad thighs against her silk-covered legs.

That Armani scent, mixed in with a smell that was all his own, grabbed her senses and hit her hard.

And the way he looked next to her…so comfortable, so pleased to have her near…well, it disturbed her more than she dared to admit. Pressing against him in the cab of his truck was all her high-school dreams come true.

Well, if you took out the disastrous date with Pete and the fact that his brother was wedged on her other side.

After about ten minutes or so, Jarred finally spoke. "So, our lesson for tonight is still on, right?"

The last thing she wanted was to trade barbs with him for another hour. Her defenses were too low.

But she couldn't say no. Not when he'd gone out of his way to try and stop Pete's roving hands. "Do you still want to?"

"I do." He paused for a second, then cleared his throat. "I

mean, since the auction is tomorrow night, I know I'm gonna need as much from you as I can get."

On Serena's other side, Cal snorted under his breath. "If today's little episode is any indication, you're gonna need a whole lot more than what Serena can give you."

In spite of her vow to stay mad at him for twenty-four hours, Serena found herself coming to his defense. "Actually, if you take out the part when Jarred told the whole restaurant Pete was grabbing my rear end, I think what he did for me this evening was kind of chivalrous."

Jarred looked pleased. "Yeah?"

"Yes." Fact was, she'd been getting a little creeped out about Pete. He'd gone from being tentative and sweet to more than a little full of himself to an octopus. The only consolation was that she now didn't feel bad for not liking him.

Because Jarred looked so interested, she opened up a little more. "Now that I think about it, the comparisons between you and Pete are pretty telling. Jarred, you might be a bit rough around the edges, but you've always treated me with respect."

Gripping the steering wheel with one hand, he reached over and brushed her cheek lightly with a knuckle. "I have."

It felt only right to take his hand and clasp it between the two of her own. "Pete, on the other hand, looks all polished and perfect. He sure knows all about the right silverware and doesn't chew with his mouth open and lets me enter doors first. But under all that, why, he's one of the rudest men I've ever encountered."

As Jarred squeezed her hand in reassurance, Cal spoke. "What exactly was his problem, anyway?"

Serena figured since they had witnessed Pete try to feel her butt, she had nothing to hide. "I don't know. It all started when he called to tell me that my bank account was overdrawn.

Then he volunteered to lend me some money. It was so nice of him to offer, I felt obligated to go out to dinner with him."

"And then he decided to press his luck." Jarred scowled. "You should have told him no to it all, Serena."

"I didn't have much of a choice. He offered to help. And he always has been a nice guy."

Still holding her hand, he squeezed it again. "Maybe he's not that nice. You know what I mean?"

Jarred's voice was full of brotherly concern. And his hand felt warm in between her own. Friendly. Oh, but she wished it could have been something more. "I know. It's just too bad, though. I was kind of hoping there might have been something between us."

His voice lowered. "Seri, honey, how much do you need?"

"I don't want to talk about it." Not while he was holding her hand. Not with Cal sitting there, too.

"Come now. We're all friends here."

Cal chimed in. "Serena, I know for a fact everyone in our house would be just sick if you were going without."

If she hedged any more, if would just get awkward. "About ninety dollars," she mumbled.

"How much, really?"

Knowing she wasn't going to get a paycheck for a bit made her double the amount. "More like two hundred. Give or take."

He rolled his eyes. "Serena, does that let you eat and fill up that car of yours, too?"

"Okay. Maybe three hundred. I'm in a little financial mess. My library pay was cut and the interest on my student loans went up. It's just about killing me," she admitted.

"Why didn't you just come over and ask for help?"

"We're friends, Jarred."

"And friends help each other out."

"I couldn't let you do that." It was one thing to give him lessons for too much money—but a whole other thing to accept a loan like that.

"I know I look like a dumb cowboy, but me and Junior have been doing all right, managing my dad's money."

"If you don't trust Jarred, come talk to me," Cal said. "I'll be happy to help get you organized."

"All right. Maybe. If you really don't mind, Cal."

"It would be my pleasure."

Jarred exhaled. "I'm glad that's settled. Tonight, we'll work on my manners. Then as soon as the auction is over, you can come over and Cal will help you out."

"Y'all will have time for that? You'll be busy with Veronica. And your father's sick, you know."

"I'll make time. It's what friends do, right?"

Friends. That's what they were. That's all they were ever going to be. "Right."

He looked pleased as he pulled into the carport and turned off the ignition. "Great. Now, let me go check on my dad and then we'll have my lesson."

As they climbed out of the car, Serena realized all she could think about was Jarred. And not a bit of it had anything to do with his manners.

SERENA WAS STANDING IN the dining room, trying to decide what to teach Jarred about place settings and dining with ladies when Jarred's little sister wandered in.

"Hi."

"Hi, to you, too, Ginny. Do you remember me? I'm Serena."

"I remember. One time you went riding with Jarred."

"That's right."

"And now you're helping my brother act more polite for Miss Veronica."

"I am. Well, I'm trying to. How do you think I'm doing so far?"

"I don't know. Okay, I guess." She walked around the table, dragging two fingers along the top as she talked. "My daddy's home sick today."

"I sure am sorry about that."

Virginia paused. "His heart's sick."

"I hope it feels better soon."

Her two thick pigtails bobbed as she nodded. "Me, too."

Eager to bring up a happier topic, Serena said, "Did you know I'm a librarian?"

"What's that?"

"I work in the library. We lend books to people. We have story time every Monday morning. You ought to come by one time."

She wrinkled her nose. "Story time's for little kids. I'm five."

"Even big kids like to read books. Do you like to read?"

"Uh-huh. I have a couple of books. Do you want to see?"

Serena looked down the hall. There was still no sign of Jarred. Most likely it would be a while, too. "Sure."

Virginia held out a hand and then led Serena up the winding staircase and down a hall. "That's Trent's room. And that one there is Junior's."

"Where's Jarred's room?" she asked before she could stop herself.

"Down that hallway. I'm over here by Gwen, when she spends the night. She's not my grandma, but I still love her."

"I'm glad about that."

They walked into a room that was full of everything horsey. As cute horseshoe border decorated pale pink walls. A spiffy bookshelf filled with Breyer horses stood in a corner. "Oh, these are pretty."

"That's my stable. I love horses." Still holding on to Serena's hand, Virginia guided her over to another bookshelf. This one was far smaller, but had a collection of hardcover picture books and seven *Penny Lane Horse Farm* books.

Serena bent down and pulled the first of the series out. "Oh, Virginia, I love these books."

"I've never read them. My mommy's mommy gave them to me."

"You ought to get someone to read you one until you learn to read."

"Maybe. The boys are real busy, though."

Serena looked out the doorway. There still wasn't a footstep to be heard. "If you want, I could read to you now."

Eagerness filled the little girl's eyes. "Really?"

"Really. I can honestly say I'd love to do nothing more."

Virginia scrambled up onto the bed. "We can sit here together."

"We sure can." With all the pomp and circumstance a new book and the beginning of a series called for, Serena opened *Penelope's Big Day* and said, "'Chapter One. Penelope Gets a New Home.'"

Chapter Fifteen

"Trent, have you seen Serena?" Jarred asked as he threw out the remains of his father's dinner. His dad had been appreciative of Jean Claude's efforts, but hadn't eaten much. After a period of unsuccessful coaxing, Jarred had given up and let him go back to sleep.

"I think she's with Virginia," Trent said, gamely taking the dirty dishes from Jarred and carrying them to the sink. "I overheard her chattering to Serena about her room. You know how that little thing loves to show off her horses."

Ever since their dad had plopped her on the back of a pony at three, Virginia loved nothing more than horses. Her toy horse collection with its own little stables and barn was her pride and joy. "I'll go check there. Thanks."

He heard Serena before he saw her cuddled up next to Virginia. The picture they made together was priceless. Serena looked completely content, lying back against layer after layer of white and pink lace. And Ginny's face showed pure bliss as she sat motionless, soaking up every word of the story.

Warmth seeped through him. For a moment, he couldn't help but imagine being with Serena. She'd bring peace and ease into his life—he knew it without a doubt. She'd read to their children and greet him with a knowing smile in their bedroom every night. Then he'd settle close to her and show her how desirable he thought she was.

Instinctively, he knew that life with Veronica wouldn't quite be like that. But surely living with her had other benefits?

When she noticed he was there, Serena stopped midsentence. "Jarred. Hi."

One blink brought him back to the present. To his goal. To what he should be hoping for. "Hey. I've been looking for y'all."

"I'm sorry. I got to talking with Virginia about her horses, and then we had to go look at them. Next thing you know, we discovered her collection of books."

"This is a really good book, Jarred," Virginia added.

Serena smiled at her fondly. "I agree, but it's time for me to go visit with your brother."

When she made a move to get up, he stopped her with a hand. "Don't. I like seeing the two of you here together." He leaned against the door frame. "And I don't think Ginny would ever forgive me if you stopped the story midsentence. I can wait a few."

Virginia clapped her hands. "Hooray! Jarred, come listen! Penelope's a horse. And she's been an orphan. She just got her own girl—but the girl's allergic to horses!"

Serena chuckled. "All that happened in the first seven pages."

"Well, now, being allergic to a horse hardly seems fair. We better see what happens next." Jarred bypassed the bed. He wasn't comfortable sitting on a bed with Serena—even with a little girl between them—and gingerly sat on Virginia's desk chair instead.

"I hope Penelope won't have to move."

"I hope so, too. But I'm only going to read these last two pages of the chapter. Then we'll have to find out about Penelope and the girl another day."

"But, Serena, you're not gonna go, are you?"

"I have to. I've got to go help your brother. I promised I'd help him."

"Oh. Okay."

Jarred knew he shouldn't be feeling guilty. After what he learned about Serena's finances, she needed all the lessons he could dream up.

Plus, there were plenty of other adults in the house. One of them could read to Virginia. When they had time.

But something about that didn't set real well with him. His conscience started pressing him about how easily they all pushed Ginny's needs to the side when there was something else to do.

All the more reason he needed a woman in the house.

"You know, we have time. Serena, if you don't mind, maybe you could read a little bit more? Now I'm a mite worried about old Penelope, too."

Virginia rose up on her knobby knees. "Oh, she's not old, Jarred. She's young and pretty."

He winked Serena's way. "Just the way I like 'em. Read a little bit more, would you, Seri, honey? I mean, if it's not too much trouble?"

Amusement entered her gaze. "I'm a librarian. It's never too much trouble to read a book."

They settled in. Before Jarred knew it, he, too, was feeling sorry for the pretty little mare who needed a good home and someone to feed her apples and carrots.

As Serena's voice floated over them, an unusual feeling of calm settled in. He liked her pretty voice. He liked how she could make all the animals in poor Penelope's makeshift barn come alive.

He especially loved the way she curved an arm around Ginny as she read. His sister surely did need as many of those feminine touches as possible.

Then, all too soon, she closed the book. "That's it for now."

"Just a little more, please, Serena?" Virginia begged around a yawn.

"Nope." Looking apologetically in his direction, her cheeks colored. "I've already interfered enough with your brother's evening. And you, my dear, are looking sleepy."

"Am not."

As Serena slid off the bed, Jarred organized the sheets around Virginia. "Even if you're not sleepy at all, I want you to try to get some sleep. We've got another riding lesson tomorrow."

"Promise."

"Uh-huh." Pressing his lips to her brow, he murmured good-night, then led Serena back downstairs and into the dining room. "From the fancy table setting, I figured this is where you want us?"

"Yes." To his amusement, Serena looked all business. "Sit here. I took the liberty of raiding your china cabinet while you were with your dad. Now we're going to pretend you're eating a four-course meal."

"My table manners are pretty good."

"Then this should be easy." She slipped an empty bowl in front of him. "Pretend that's soup. Which spoon will you use?"

Even he knew it was the big one. But perversely, he picked up the teaspoon just to rile her up. "This?"

"No. That's the teaspoon for coffee," she patiently corrected. Leaning close, she pointed to the soup spoon. "This is the one you should be using. See how the bowl of the spoon is a little bigger? More round? That's how you can tell it's for soup."

Her hair smelled like the honeysuckle vines in his mother's old rose arbor. Feminine and sweet.

Blindly, he picked up the spoon.

"Very good." Picking up the bowl, she scurried to the server at the end of the dining room and pulled out a salad plate.

Though he certainly enjoyed her jeans, seeing Serena in a royal-blue wraparound dress was something to see. That shiny knit fabric hugged every single delicious curve and practically invited him to hug her, too.

"Now you're having salad. Which fork?"

There were three in front of him. This time, he really had no clue. Taking a chance, he picked up the one the farthest out.

She beamed. "Good job!"

"Thanks."

And so it continued.

It should have been boring. He should have been starving— he never did get a chance to eat anything. Or she should have been irritating with her prissy ways and advice.

Instead, he found himself listening and trying. Just to see her smile with delight.

Now that there were no little girls between them or brothers sitting nearby, it became hard to think about anything but Serena. He was very aware of her scent. Of the nape of her neck. Of the way she tilted her head when she was thinking hard.

And of how her eyes sparkled when he teased her.

For a few minutes at a time, he even found himself forgetting to concentrate on the reason he was doing everything. About Veronica and her fashion-model body and high-class ways.

He forgot about the thrill he was expecting to have when she chose him for the auction. The pride he knew he'd feel when he squired her around town—never mind that he was bought and paid for and the whole thing was simply for a good cause.

Suddenly, he was only thinking about Serena and those lips of hers.

And how she'd react if he pulled her onto his lap and kissed her like crazy next time she leaned over and tossed him with a glimpse of generous cleavage.

All too soon, she looked at her watch. "Oh! Our time is up."

But he wasn't ready for her to go. "Want to hang around for a bit? I could pour you a glass of wine."

"Thanks, but it's getting late, and I've got to open up the library at nine tomorrow morning."

"Then let me at least give you this." After putting a couple of folded bills in her hand, he said, "Please let me help you out, Serena. We are friends, you know. And I promised…"

"I know. You don't go back on your promises."

"You'll let me?"

"Let's see how you feel about it on Monday."

"Why Monday?"

"Because it will be your first day with whoever buys you, remember? The auction is tomorrow night."

The auction. Veronica. The perfect, blue-blooded society gal he wanted to have as part of the family. "Oh, yeah. Well, I won't change my mind."

"I'll talk to you then." She touched his arm. "And, uh, Jarred?"

"Yeah?"

"Thanks for today. Thanks for hitting Pete and offering to help me out. I really appreciate it." Leaning up on her tiptoes, she raised her head to kiss his cheek.

Instinctively, he bent down to let her do that. But then before he knew it, he moved his head and met her lips with his.

And kissed her again.

Just like in the library, her lips were soft. But this time, there was no shock between them, only the silent knowledge that what they were doing was inevitable.

Gently he brushed his lips over hers, familiarizing himself again, coaxing them open. And then deepening that kiss.

Oh, but she tasted like vanilla and sweetness. He wrapped his arms around her and pulled her closer. To his delight, she moved in, pressing against him.

He splayed a hand at her waist. Tried to be a gentleman. But when she wiggled a little closer, stretching her arms and pressing close, his right hand slid a little lower and cupped her bottom.

He nibbled her bottom lip, then teased her mouth open again. With a moan, she raised her hands to his hair. His other hand wandered to her hip. And still they kissed.

His brain became fuzzy as age-old instincts took over and he got to know her jawline. The nape of her neck. When she placed a palm on his chest, he moved one of his to her rib cage.

Her breath hitched.

He stepped back to get some more room…then realized he was in the dining room. With Serena. His buddy.

Who'd just been manhandled by the banker.

Shocked, he pulled away.

Wide-eyed, she stared at him. "I'm so sorry."

Unable to help himself, he moved a thumb along the outline of her lips. Noticed that his five-o'clock shadow had abraded the skin a bit. "Why are you sorry? Sweetheart, I'm the one who kissed you."

"I know but…"

He reached for her hand. Threaded her fingers with his own. "Maybe we should talk about this?" He was no Dr. Phil, but it did feel as though they were in for a relationship train wreck.

"No. There's nothing to talk about. I better go."

Because he wasn't exactly sure how he was feeling about everything, he let her.

Chapter Sixteen

"I'd say this VFW hall looks pretty good all dolled up," Tracy stated when she joined Serena over at the punch bowl on Saturday night at seven o'clock. "It's going to look even better when we get the money to spruce it up some, too."

"The new tile floor is sorely needed."

"As is landscaping outside," Tracy mused. "Of course my favorite purchase is going to be the tree we're going to plant in honor of war veterans."

Serena liked the idea of knowing that she'd had some part in that memorial. "I sure hope we get enough money for everything on the list."

"I think we will. Veronica called up a bunch of her Dallas girlfriends, and they brought some friends. Every one of them seems to think one-hundred-dollar bills are the same as ones. They're spending like crazy."

"At least someone has money to spare," Serena said drily. "How's the silent-auction part going? I've been manning the refreshment table for the past half hour since I got here. I haven't been able to take a look."

"It's going great. So far, there's at least two hundred dollars bid on everything. Some have as much as a thousand." Her eyes lit up. "And the regular auction is fixing to start. That's what I came over to tell you."

An uneasy flutter filled her stomach, though she didn't

know its source. Was she nervous about Jarred not doing well—or anxious that he was about to get what he wanted?

She supposed only time would tell.

Looking at the punch bowl and the bottles of soda, she reached down into the plastic crate by her feet and pulled out a few more glasses. "I'll just get this a little more organized then see if someone can take my place."

Tracy slipped an arm through hers. "Don't worry so much. This area is fine. If there's anything this crowd knows how to do, it's how to serve themselves drinks. Come sit down."

"All right." She supposed her nonalcoholic punch wouldn't get overrun by takers anytime soon, anyway. Everyone present was lining up at the cash bar and drinking Lone Star and Budweiser as if it was going out of style.

After filling four more glasses, she put the ladle down and followed Tracy to the third row of white fold-out chairs. As Serena looked around at the seating arrangement, she had to smile. It looked almost exactly as if it was set up for a wedding—eight rows of chairs on each side of a wide aisle.

In front of everything was a raised dais for all the people offering services to stand on. The Boy Scouts had built it. They'd hung up an extra-large bulletin board behind it, as well.

Mayor Earl was standing behind a podium over to the right. Standing tall and proud as ever, he experimentally banged his gavel for silence and spoke into the microphone borrowed from the Presbyterian church. "Let's get ready to rumble!" he called out in his best sports-announcer imitation.

"Oh, brother," Tracy said. "I swear, our mayor gets a little more eccentric with every passing year."

As Mayor Earl started tapping the microphone and tested the volume, Serena smiled. "I wouldn't have it any other way."

Moments later, the gavel rang out again. "I hereby proclaim

this auction begun! Let's take a look-see at item number one." He shifted his gaze to the left. "Paula, show this crowd what we've got."

Tracy giggled. "He sounds like Bob Barker."

"Almost," Serena agreed, then tamped down her overactive sweet tooth as she watched Paula present her offering, a dish of ice cream every week for two months.

"Two months! Why, that's eight free ice creams, y'all," Mayor Earl proclaimed.

Tracy giggled. And then the bidding began.

AN HOUR LATER, SERENA looked at her program. Jarred was almost the last thing to be auctioned. He was listed under *Bonus and Once in a Lifetime Experiences.* There in black and white, Serena saw that A Week with Jarred Riddell was number forty-nine, smack between an all-expense-paid trip to Kauai and the chance to be the lead story on the front page of the *Electra Enquirer Newspaper.*

She shook her head wryly. It was a sure bet that Jarred's ego was having a field day with that one!

As Mayor Earl started bidding on item number twenty-five—cookies for a year by Mrs. Anderson—Serena looked around.

She knew most everyone. There with her mother was Veronica Snow. She was looking like a model out of a magazine, dressed as she was in a gorgeous sundress with tiny spaghetti straps. Not too far off were Cal Jr. and Trent Riddell. Sitting with them was Gwen. On her lap was little Virginia.

Near the front was Jean Claude Valentine. She knew he was auctioning off a free dinner at the Golden Dove. The Hendersons were there from the bakery, and now that her item was bid on and signed, Paula was back at work, scooping ice cream for the crowd.

Finally, in the back of the room she spotted Jarred. The

sight of him took her breath away. He looked drop-dead gorgeous in his tuxedo. Honestly, for a man who hardly ever wore a clean shirt, he sure looked like a movie star in a tuxedo. It fit him so well, one would think it had been designed and tailored just for him.

He wasn't smiling. No, he was standing quietly, sipping a glass of water.

She wondered what he was thinking.

"Serena, stop squirming and look at the mayor," Tracy whispered. "He's about to auction off a whole assortment of Mary Kay!"

Obediently, Serena turned to the front. But though the makeup in its pretty pink boxes looked nice, she couldn't help but wonder about Jarred. And wonder what was going to happen to him. When she looked Veronica's way again, Serena noticed that there was an empty seat next to her. Serena decided to claim it. Just in case ol' Veronica needed some coaxing where Jarred Riddell was concerned.

Because the only thing worse than seeing Jarred take Veronica out on dates for one whole week was to have him not get the girl of his dreams at all.

AS BAD IDEAS WENT, LETTING himself be an auctioned bachelor had to be one of his very worst, Jarred decided as Mayor Earl called him to the front of the room.

Remembering Serena's instructions about walking slowly, he ambled down the center aisle.

Hell. He felt like a freakin' bride.

Two old guys from the hardware store guffawed as he passed. So did Chrissy from the Pizza Whiz. He'd never felt so humiliated.

He didn't dare let it show, though. He playfully gave the old guys the finger and winked at Chrissy when she whistled at his butt.

"Step right up, Jarred!" Mayor Earl proclaimed. "Ladies, if you were ever wondering if Electra could compete with those cheesy bachelors on the television, I'm asking you to look no further. This guy has it all—good looks, fun personality and that impressive Riddell name. And did I mention that he's rich?"

If the crowd hadn't been going wild before, it sure was now. And the suggestions the boys from Ed's Feed and Seed were calling out had to surely come from too much Budweiser.

"That ain't physically possible, Ed," he sniped right back... even as he felt his ears turn red. Virginia really shouldn't be hearing such things.

But the ribbing continued.

"How do you know it ain't possible?" Trent yelled from his chair.

Oh, Lord. He was going to kill his little brother. "'Cause I've tried it, that's why!"

Laughter erupted and he posed and grinned. Playing along as though he was having the time of his life.

But he wasn't.

Actually, Jarred didn't think he could feel more of a fool if he was standing there stark naked. He was half surprised the mayor didn't ask him to show off his teeth.

"Jarred, why don't you tell the women out here what you plan to do with the winner."

"Anything they want," he drawled. When a whole assortment of hoots and hollers accompanied that, he felt his cheeks heat. "I mean, within reason."

He scanned the audience, intent on finding Veronica. But when his eyes lit on Serena, he couldn't seem to look away. She was gazing at him with enough trust and comfort to make him feel as if he could do anything.

And it served to settle him, too. He knew how to play up his good ol' boy roots. And, if he were honest, standing in front of the town in a too-hot tuxedo was a whole hell of a lot easier than facing the wild-eyed glare of an ornery bull with a hump on its back in Cheyenne.

Because it was expected, he lifted his chin and deepened his drawl when the mayor prodded him to talk some more. "One thing I was planning to do was take the lucky woman to dinner at the Golden Dove. I also hope to take her horseback riding down in the valley, and finish off the day with a picnic by the river."

With a knowing glance at the audience, Mayor Earl said, "And what about that famous Corvette? Any rides in that?"

"Of course." Thinking quickly, Jarred said, "We'll go anywhere she wants in that car. As long as I'm driving, of course."

As the room filled with whistles and good-natured laughter, the mayor tapped his gavel on the podium and announced, "Let's start the bidding at one hundred dollars. Do I hear one hundred?"

Jarred scanned the crowd and looked at his brothers, who were grinning ear to ear. Looked at his other friends sipping longnecks and giving him the thumbs-up.

His gaze found Serena and their eyes locked. And found a little thread of warmth glide through him when he read her lips, telling him "good job." Everything was going to be just fine. And then he realized—much to his surprise—that she was keeping company with Veronica Snow.

Chapter Seventeen

Mayor Earl banged on the gavel again. "Hey, y'all. The fire chief needs to ask me a question. This is just going to take a sec. Jarred, cool your heels for a moment, why don't you?"

As the mayor left the stage and Jarred stood there all alone, the butterflies in Serena's stomach fluttered nervously.

Oh, this was going to be a disaster.

Serena felt like a nervous mother at her daughter's first dance. Her palms were sweating, her pulse was accelerated and her stomach was in knots. Everything that was most important to her was on display.

With some dismay, she realized that though some things changed, others stayed completely the same. Jarred Riddell still had her heart—and she loved him enough to hope that he was about to get everything he ever wanted.

It was just a shame that what he wanted was Veronica Snow.

With a sinking heart, Serena watched Veronica hop up from the chair beside her and go talk to some of her friends. As Serena watched Jarred watch Veronica, she mentally started practicing all the things she was going to tell Veronica in order to encourage her to bid.

"Serena, you look worried enough to burst into tears, right here in row number five. You've got to settle down," Tracy said as she scooted closer.

"I'm just trying to come up with the right thing to say so she'll bid on Jarred."

"I doubt you'll need to worry. If she's not thinking about all the fun, private things she could do to Jarred Riddell's person, she's surely the only person with two ovaries who isn't! Every woman between twelve and ninety-two is staring at Jarred and salivating."

It didn't help that she knew exactly what a good kisser Jarred was. Yes, some lucky woman was going to have quite a time cuddled in his arms.

But though jealousy was threatening to make her crazy, Serena couldn't help but feel a real case of pride as she watched Jarred grin on that stage. He looked confident and, well, debonair! She'd earned every penny of what he paid her. "He does look good, doesn't he?"

"Good enough to eat."

"I wish Mayor Earl would come back. Don't you think he's been gone long enough?"

"Patience, little sister," Tracy said in parting as Veronica returned to take her seat.

It was time to plant some seeds.

"Having a good time, Veronica?"

"Definitely. You?"

"Of course. Um, I was just sitting here, thinking about Jarred. He looks real good, doesn't he?"

Veronica turned to stare at the man of the hour. "He is handsome." She leaned in and lowered her voice. "But between you and me, I don't understand why anyone would even want to pay a dollar for his time."

Uh-oh. "Veronica, I've been friends with Jarred for years. I've got to tell you, you'll never find a better man than him."

"You really think that, don't you? Don't you think he's a little rough around the edges?"

"Only enough to make him interesting. I mean, who would want a guy who was too polished, you know?"

Veronica stared at him again. This time a little bit longer. With a little bit more interest. "You might have a point there."

"You know, I think it's also great that it's just for a week. If you don't like him, there won't be any of those awkward breakups."

"That's true. I never thought about it that way."

Jarred was still standing all by himself like a target. Everyone was staring at him and whispering. Whispering so quietly, she couldn't overhear much at all.

"I'm back. Sorry about that," Mayor Earl boomed. "Take your seats, please, and direct your attention back to Electra's own Jarred Riddell. For those of you who don't know him personally, let me just say he's a former rodeo star, semiconfirmed bachelor and all-around good person." A sly grin lit his face. "And, we sure can't forget that he's a great addition to any party. I've never met a man more able to schmooze and booze than Jarred."

Serena's stomach sank as she watched the muscles in Jarred's jaw jump. She knew for a fact that he hated being reduced to nothing more than a party guy.

"You ready, Jarred?"

Her student lifted his head and looked out into the audience. Their eyes met once again. His were blue and piercing. Her own tried their best to convey her hopes for him—and that she was sure this little bit of humiliation was going to be totally worth it.

Then he turned to the mayor and grinned that trademark smile of his. "Absolutely."

"Then let's get this show on the road." Mayor Earl cleared his throat. "Don't forget, this is for charity, y'all. Your monies are going to benefit everyone young and old. We're going to fix up this VFW hall and maybe even help the firehouse a bit. So…do I hear one hundred?"

Now it was so quiet everyone could hear old Mr. Palmer snoring near the punch bowl.

Mayor Earl tapped the microphone. "Fifty, anyone?"

Serena gulped. *Fifty?* She had been sure women were going to be throwing money the mayor's way. Diverting her eyes to Jarred, she saw that muscle in his jaw twitch again.

Oh, but he was agitated.

Oh, but she was up a creek. Nothing she'd done had worked! Not her lessons, not her reconnaissance!

The mayor tapped the microphone experimentally. "Forty?"

A muffled voice in the back row called out, "All right, Earl. I'll bid. Forty."

People clapped and cheered.

Serena turned quickly and half rose out of her chair, trying to figure out who called out the bid, but there was so much commotion, she couldn't tell.

Mayor Earl smiled. "Forty it is, to the lady in the back. Do I hear fifty?"

"We'll bid one hundred dollars, Mayor," one of the gals from the Burger Shack called out. "But Jarred's going to have to work for all three of us. That is, if he can handle us."

Trent Riddell whistled raucously.

Jarred winked. "I can handle ya'll just fine."

"Be still my heart," one church lady behind Serena murmured. "What a man that is. I bet he's heaven in bed."

Serena gasped. That woman had to be almost ninety! She certainly gave a new meaning to the term *cougar.* Kind of meanly, Serena began to think of other names to describe her such an old *cat.*

But Mayor Earl didn't look shocked by the bid—or the

crazy comments bandied about—at all. Actually, he started to look a whole lot happier.

"A hundred it is! Now, do I have another bid?" Looking around, his eyes sparkled. "Come on, ladies, our Jarred is surely one of the finest that Electra has to offer. Look at that physique!"

Dutifully Jarred flexed a bicep.

A couple of guys in the audience whistled and called out all kinds of things that really shouldn't be said in mixed company.

That darn lady behind her made little gasping noises.

Serena delicately nudged Veronica. "He's a good guy, Veronica. The best. You ought to bid."

"You think?"

"I know."

Mayor Earl spoke again. "Once more, your money will go to help all kinds of needs in the community. Think how nice this place is going to look with new carpeting. Think of the orphans!"

Orphans? Oh, brother. While Serena certainly didn't begrudge a cent going to anyone needy, she happened to know for a fact that there was no orphanage within a hundred-mile radius.

Whether it was the idea of Jarred getting farmed out to groups of women—or the sympathy factor in full force because of the orphans—bidding started picking up.

Mayor Earl's voice got peppier and louder as bids came in from all over the crowd. "One-fifty. Two hundred. Two-fifty. Five hundred."

Two rows over, Hannah fanned herself. "Five hundred dollars is a lot of money to spend on a man."

"It is," a few others agreed.

"I wonder what a person would get for that much? I wonder what ol' Jarred would do?"

Serena turned to Veronica one last time. "Are you going to bid? Or is a date with Jarred going to be just another thing you wish you would have done?"

Veronica blinked. "I have wasted a lot of time with regrets." She leaned forward.

Serena nodded. "Go on, Veronica. Bid."

But right as Veronica looked as if she was about to bid, the rest of the women in the audience went berserk. In a space of ten seconds, offers started pouring in.

"I have five-fifty! Six hundred. No, wait…seven hundred. One thousand! One thousand dollars. Woo-wee!"

It was thrilling. Jarred had to be excited about the money being raised. But as she caught his eye, she knew his smile was merely pasted on.

He wasn't happy. He was bummed. She couldn't help but feel a tiny bit devastated for his sake, too. Not a one of those bids had been from their token society belle. Yep, all the while, Veronica Snow had been suspiciously silent.

Even Serena's poor job of egging her on hadn't done a bit of good.

"One thousand and ten? Anyone? Anyone at all?"

Silence.

Mayor Earl seemed to know when enough was enough. "All righty, then. Here we go. One thousand dollars going once. Going twice…" He lifted the gavel.

The whole crowd braced themselves for a crashing pound—

"Two thousand dollars!"

Mayor Earl's hand froze.

Serena's mouth dropped open as she looked to her right. Veronica Snow was standing up and waving her hand like nobody's business.

Jarred Riddell's smile suddenly became three feet wide.

Veronica Snow had just bid two thousand dollars on Jarred Riddell, the most eligible bachelor in town.

Without further ado, Mayor Earl banged the podium. "Sold!"

"Holy Toledo!" Hannah exclaimed.

Trent and Cal Jr. got to their feet and high-fived each other.

Grinning like a fox in the henhouse, Mayor Earl reached over and clasped Jarred's shoulders. "Congratulations, man! Jarred, you have just been sold for two thousand dollars! Lord have mercy. What do you say to that?"

Casually, as if he was moving in slow motion, Jarred approached the microphone. A hush filled the arena.

Standing tall, looking movie-star handsome, he grinned. Women all around Serena sighed. "Well, Mayor Earl, I say that Veronica Snow just got herself a heck of a deal," he drawled. "I intend to make Miss Snow's purchase worth every penny."

A burst of applause rang out as the men shouted unrepeatable phrases and the women pretended to be offended. Serena couldn't help it, she smiled up at Jarred. So pleased for him.

But he wasn't looking her way. Not any longer.

No, he only had eyes for the vision who stood up, then started walking his way in the prettiest floral sundress Serena had ever seen. Cut like something a 1950s Grace Kelly would wear, the vibrant floral print hugged her torso then flared out in a full skirt. "There has to be tulle under the skirt of that dress," Hannah whispered. "It's that full."

"It's absolutely beautiful," Serena agreed, thinking enviously that only a woman with no hips could pull it off. That kind of dress on her figure would look as if she'd put on a boat.

"I heard she bought that dress in New York City two weekends ago," Hannah whispered. "It's *designer*."

The silky dress flounced around Veronica's calves as she

continued down the aisle, passing the lot of them without a backward glance.

As Veronica approached the stage, Mayor Earl almost tripped over himself trying to help her up the steps.

But then Jarred took her hand and wrapped an arm around her waist. She lifted her chin, wrapped one manicured hand around his neck and whispered something. His eyes widened, he whispered something back, then right there and then, Jarred lowered his head and slowly, methodically, kissed her.

Right there. On the stage. In front of everyone!

And as if she were witnessing a train wreck, Serena couldn't stop staring. That kiss was so picture-perfect, it looked like something out of an old MGM musical. Or *Pretty Woman.*

"Now that, everyone, is what a two-thousand-dollar kiss looks like!" Mayor Earl declared.

"Two thousand dollars is a helluva lot of money!" Trent called out. "You better do it again."

Jarred laughed. Veronica smiled. And then he swung her up in his arms and kissed her again.

As clapping and laughter floated up again, Serena wished she could sink to the floor. Because all she could notice when she watched Jarred kiss Veronica, was that it looked a whole lot like the kiss he gave her.

Just the night before.

Back when she'd been fooling herself into thinking that maybe there was more between them than she'd ever thought possible.

Chapter Eighteen

After everyone went home from the VFW, Serena stayed late to help with the cleanup. Then she'd shared a piece of cake with a few other volunteers. Finally, a little after midnight, she went on home.

Oh, she'd had offers to do other things. A few girls had invited her to the Burger Shack for a late-night meal and a few rounds of beer.

Tracy had asked Serena to spend the night at her house. Even Hannah had invited her to her apartment for tea.

But Serena knew she couldn't listen to any more talk about Veronica and Jarred for another minute. No, all she wanted to do was go home and try to decompress.

If that was even possible.

Her apartment was dark when she entered. When she turned on the hall light, it only served to remind her of how much she'd been neglecting her housework ever since she'd started tutoring Jarred. Resolutely ignoring the dishes in the sink, Serena kicked off her shoes and curled up on the couch.

Oh, she couldn't believe the auction was over.

While they'd been throwing away trash and stacking chairs, more than a few people had come by to congratulate her on Jarred's awesome performance. He'd impressed many with his ease in that tuxedo, and with the way he had acted that evening, opening doors and pulling out chairs for women.

Lots of people gave her a heap of credit for taming the oldest Riddell. For changing him into something almost reputable. For making him attractive enough for the fanciest of women.

Serena had smiled her thanks but had refused any responsibility for Jarred's success. "He really didn't need my help," she'd said. "He's always been someone our town should be proud of. I'm sure Veronica will enjoy his company and the town will enjoy the benefits."

Everyone said she shouldn't be so modest.

But Serena knew the truth. Truth was, Jarred had done all that on his own. He hadn't needed her to make him better. To her, he'd always been good enough. He'd simply been a little rough around the edges.

Now that she was back home and sitting alone with nothing to look forward to except a load of bills, Serena felt more depressed than she had in years. Before those lessons, she'd been happy with her life. Before being around Jarred so much, she'd come to terms that their lives would always be parallel to each other. That there was no reason for them to intersect.

But now things felt different. She was different. She wanted more than just a library job, a tiny apartment and a bunch of good girlfriends.

Seeing Jarred obtain his dream made her wish she could make some of her dreams happen, too.

Walking to her kitchen, she opened a bottle of merlot and poured herself a generous glass, then picked up her reading glasses and one of the books from the to-be-read stack.

She sat by the window and tried not to think about Jarred and Veronica being together at that very moment. Tried not to imagine him kissing her.

Actually, she tried not to care.

"WHATCHA DOING TODAY, Jarred?" Virginia asked when she wandered into his room the morning after the auction.

"Sleeping," he mumbled. "Ginny, it's early, honey."

"Not so early. Daddy said it was a quarter past ten."

He opened one eye. "That late, huh?" When her curls bobbed with her nod, he sat up with a groan. Though his head felt fuzzy from the bottle of champagne he and Veronica had shared, he patted the side of his bed so Ginny could climb up. She did, her red polka-dot pajamas sliding up to midcalf as she scooted close.

"Do you want to go riding with me?"

"I don't know if I can, squirt. I've got to tend to the horses."

"Trent already did that."

"That was nice of him." As his bleary eyes focused, he thought some more. "I also have to see what Miss Veronica wants to do today, too. I'm going to be on her schedule for the next week."

"Because she bought you?"

That sounded almost dirty to him. "Well, she bid on me for charity. She didn't actually buy me."

"Trent says you have to do whatever she wants, but then after the week is done, you won't get to see her no more."

"Anymore," he corrected, then blinked in surprise. Since when did he correct grammar? "And don't listen to Trent. I might see Miss Veronica a whole lot more, even when I don't have to."

"So, you like spending time with her?"

Remembering how pretty she was sitting across from him sipping champagne, he smiled. "Of course."

"Why?"

"Why? Because she's beautiful."

"Are you going to bring her by?"

"Maybe." But even as he promised, Jarred wasn't sure if he

would bring Veronica by anytime soon. He wasn't sure how she'd react to being around his brothers. After all, he was the only one of them who'd had any formal training.

Virginia wiggled around until her face was almost touching his. "Do you think she'll want to read with me?"

"I don't know."

"Why not? Does she like books?"

"I don't know that answer, either. I'm just getting to know Veronica now. It takes time." Thinking about Serena, and how well he knew her, he nodded. "Shoot. Maybe even years."

Ginny scrambled off the bed. Practically reading his mind, she said, "I know! We can ask Serena to come back. She likes to read Penelope books with me."

"I don't think so."

"But I thought y'all were friends."

"We are." With effort, he pushed the sweet memory of listening to Serena read to Ginny aside. "It's just…I have Veronica now."

"And I got no one to read Penelope with," Ginny said as she left.

Guilt washed over him. He knew the right thing to do would be to get dressed and go spend some time with his little sister.

But there was so much going on in his head, all that seemed possible was to lean back against the pillows and try to get his bearings.

So much had happened over the past forty-eight hours. Saving Serena from Pete Ross. Kissing her in the moonlight.

Standing in front of the whole town in that monkey suit.

He wouldn't admit it to just anybody, but the truth was, he'd been sweating bullets up there, waiting to see if anyone was going to pay a dime to be in the same room with him.

And when old Mrs. Clare—who had to be ninety if she was

a day—had volunteered a measly forty bucks, he'd thought his goose was cooked.

But everything had changed a hundred-and-eighty degrees when Veronica had bought him. Hearing her words, seeing the approval and shock in everyone else's eyes had been especially gratifying.

He still couldn't believe what had happened next. When she'd hopped on the stage, he'd been fully prepared to twirl her around. But when he reached over to pick her up, she'd asked him to kiss her.

And he'd never been one to refuse such a request. So, he'd placed his lips on hers and held on tight. He'd kissed her like he'd dreamed of doing. Gently. With honor.

But that hadn't been what she'd wanted. Next thing he'd known, her tongue had been in his mouth and their heat was sizzling up the tent.

It had been nice.

But it had also felt impersonal and more than a little empty.

So different from when he'd kissed Serena. That had been full of surprises. When he'd wrapped his arms around her and kissed her, it had felt tender. Sweet. So secret and special.

Why was that? How come he couldn't stop thinking about her all of the sudden, now that he had everything he ever wanted?

After a brief knock, Gwen poked her head in. "Jarred, your father is calling for you."

"Tell him I'll be right there. I've just got to get dressed."

Fifteen minutes later, he let himself into his father's room. "Dad?"

His father was sitting on his couch, fully dressed in jeans and a button-down shirt and boots. "Hey, son."

"You're all dressed. You okay?"

"Well enough to want to get out of this room for a spell. I was kind of hoping you'd have time to take me."

Jarred was on the verge of second-guessing him. Of asking if that was the smart thing to do. But a lifetime of being his father's son stopped the question in its tracks. People didn't second-guess Cal Riddell. Certainly not his sons. During his whole life, Jarred had never questioned his father. He certainly wasn't about to start now.

He stepped forward. "I'll take you wherever you want to go." After helping him to his feet, he gripped his father's arm and slowly guided him down the hall. "Got somewhere special in mind?"

"Nowhere far. I just need a change of scenery."

"The rose arbor?"

His father's steps slowed. A moment passed before he replied. "That would be fine."

As they continued down the hall and into the kitchen, Jarred kept a hand free just in case his dad needed extra help. But after the first few faltering steps, he seemed to regain his balance. They walked through the sunroom without any ill effects. But when Jarred opened the back door and faced the three stone steps that provided the transition from home to garden, his father stopped.

"You okay, Dad?"

"I'm fine." Looking straight ahead, he murmured, "Just… help me with the steps, would you?"

"Sure." He grabbed his dad's elbow with one hand, and placed another around his shoulders. He was glad his father was the type of man to remain stoic. Jarred was struggling to do the same, though he couldn't help but reflect on how different his father felt under his thin long-sleeved T-shirt. Where there used to be solid muscle, Jarred now felt only a thin layer of skin covering bones. His dad had lost a lot of weight.

Finally, they sat down on cushioned chairs with sighs of relief. Jarred sat across from his father, resting his elbows on his thighs, ready to jump up to get him anything.

But Cal Sr. only looked relaxed. Tension eased from around his eyes. After closing them for a bit, he breathed deeply. "This is better. I didn't think I could take another blasted minute staring at those same four walls."

"I've always liked this patio. Mom liked it, too, I remember."

"Oh, yes, she did. I didn't at the time, though."

"Why was that?"

"Because times were so different. Trent was only six or seven, and was as busy as you ever saw. Your mother was running ragged, trying to keep up with him. With all of you. I thought she was doing too much."

Jarred tried to recall his mother being exhausted, but he couldn't. "Mom liked to be busy, didn't she?"

"She did." He cleared his throat. "Truth was, I was the one with the problem. I had been on the road so much, touring with the rodeo circuit, trying to be a star." He rolled his eyes. "All I wanted to do when I got home was watch television. Not make patios."

Listening to his father, Jarred once again realized just how much time had passed…and how things in their lives had changed.

"Jarred, the patio isn't why I wanted you to take me out here."

"Why did you?"

"I wanted to talk to you for a bit. About that auction. About Veronica. Between the phone calls and your brothers' reports…I heard quite a bit about it."

Jarred knew that was disapproval in his father's tone. For the first time, he was embarrassed at what he'd done. "It was no big deal. Just an auction for charity, Dad."

"Don't talk to me like I'm addled, boy. I know what it was. I want to know why you wanted Veronica so badly."

"She bid on me."

"With a lot of help from you." His voice deepened. "You spent hours with Serena Higgens and those crazy lessons. And during it all, I kept my mouth shut. But through it all, I never actually heard why you wanted Veronica."

"Sure, you did. We talked about how she's part of society, Dad. She's high-class."

"So?"

"So, I thought you wanted me dating someone like Veronica. She's a classy lady. Plus, someone like Veronica would be good for Ginny. She needs a woman's influence."

"I want you to be happy. If she's the one for you, then it's all good. But, is she?"

"I'm not sure." Jarred's cheeks heated. "I guess I'll find out when we spend time together."

Looking him over, his dad's eyes narrowed. "High society don't mean much over the breakfast table, son—or in the bedroom, if you get my drift."

Before Jarred could react to that, his father continued. "Actually, I have to say that once upon a time I had real high hopes for you boys…but I never intended to make y'all into something you weren't. Sometimes you simply need to look for love."

"Is that what happened with you and Mom? Love?"

"Yep. At first, though, she wasn't who I thought I wanted. I had my sights set on someone else entirely at first." He stretched his legs out and tilted his face up to the sun. "It just goes to show you, sometimes the person you think you want isn't the one who's right for you."

"I'll remember that."

"I hope so. Sometimes it's a person like Serena who catches you off guard."

"Serena and I only had a business deal." But even as he said the words, Jarred felt his ears turn red. They'd had a whole lot more than business between them for years.

"Seems that's all you have with Veronica. After all, she bought you. That's it."

"It might turn into more."

"It might. Then again, it might not. And if it doesn't, then where will you be?"

Jarred didn't have the answer to that.

Chapter Nineteen

Veronica looked so good in his Corvette, Jarred couldn't help but gloat. "Where would you like to go today, beautiful?"

To his surprise, instead of melting at his endearment, she merely looked bored. "I hate it when people say things like that. I hate false speaking."

He'd never heard the term. "Say again?"

"Come on, you know what I mean. Don't call me some generic name." Before he could apologize—though for what he wasn't quite sure—she continued. "Now, as for today, I have quite a few things on my list. First, I was hoping we could go to Hebron. There's a good salon there. I need to get my hair and nails done. Then there's a cute little boutique I want to stop in. I really need a new pair of shoes. Is that okay with you?"

"I'll do whatever you want. But, um, I had been under the impression that you wanted to spend time with me. You know, so we could get to know each other."

"Oh, I do. It's just that for once I wasn't going to have to worry about what my date wanted."

"Come again?"

"Well, I mean…I bought your time, right? So, I want to spend our time together doing what I want." She eyed him carefully. "Does that make sense?"

She asked the question doubtfully, as if he wasn't none too smart. "Of course it does," he murmured.

But though he was struggling to keep his expression interested and sweet, inside Jarred was reeling. He'd thought Veronica had really liked him.

Shoot, after that kiss, he'd thought she'd been pretty much lusting after him something awful!

Now, it seemed that she had spent two grand to get a glorified errand boy.

It sounded like hell. And, actually, it sounded a little disappointing, too. He'd enjoyed thinking she was perfect all the time. He didn't want to think about her needing hair help.

But he wasn't about to complain. Although he'd imagined Veronica wanting to use him for far more intimate reasons, he supposed no woman could look as pretty as she did without a good amount of help.

"All right, honey. Whatever you want to do is fine by me. I'll start driving and you direct me where you want to go."

But instead of simpering, like the Burger Shack girls usually did, or groaning and teasing him back, like Serena would have done, Veronica just looked irritated.

"Honestly, Jarred. My name is *Veronica*. Not sweetheart. Not beautiful. Not honey bun. Please remember to call me that."

"I'll do my best," he bit out. Unable to stop himself, he said, "Just for the record, I've never called a woman honey bun."

With as much grace as he could muster, he opened the passenger-side door of his car and stood at attention while she slid in. When she sat facing forward, just waiting for him to close that door and get in his side, Jarred started feeling a tad irritated himself.

She never even said thank-you. Serena would've given her what-for for that faux pas!

The road to Hebron was long. When he'd kissed her last

night, he'd imagined them doing all kinds of things today. When she'd asked if he'd pick her up at ten so they could run a few errands, why, he'd thought that was code for going parking.

But now that they were on the highway, their conversation was definitely strained. She didn't like his country stations.

Matter of fact, she didn't seem to like any music playing at all. No, she liked the cab quiet so they could talk.

But then she wasn't really saying much because she wasn't chatting about anything. She was more just sitting there like a bump on a log. And what was even stranger was that he couldn't think of a thing to say, either. With Serena, he could talk about everything and anything—even with the radio on.

Desperate, he said, "Tell me about your work in Dallas, sugar. I mean, Veronica."

"It was very fulfilling. I worked with a lot of nonprofits and really felt like I was making a difference. Once, we raised enough funds at a charity ball and auction to buy an ambulance."

"An ambulance? That seems like an odd thing to want to buy."

"It was for some rural communities." Her voice softened, letting him know that the cause really did mean a lot to her. "I'm told that ambulance has been responsible for saving a number of lives."

"I'm impressed."

"I didn't do all that much, Jarred. I merely helped coordinate things. I didn't raise or donate all the money, and I certainly can't do what the emergency medical technicians do."

"No, I suppose not." He knew his voice sounded deflated, but he couldn't help himself. This Veronica he was driving around was about as much fun as managing an ornery bull at roundup. Drumming his fingers on the steering wheel, he began to wonder just how many hours she was going to want him around each day.

If every conversation was as stilted, he hoped she got the flu or something.

"Hebron is this next exit."

Annoyance bubbled at the edges of his composure. "I've lived here a long time, honey. I know where Hebron is."

"I just didn't want you to miss it."

"I didn't."

Up went her chin. "Our first stop is Anderson's Hair Designs." She pointed to a quaint building that was full of frills and white lace. "See those parking places in front? Park in one of them."

Being around all that white lace was going to give him the willies. "How about I drop you off? I could come back in an hour."

"No way. I bought and paid for you! Now I'm determined to show you off. Park and let's go."

He parked and followed her in.

Lord have mercy, but the place was just as awful as he'd feared. Within seconds, four heavily made-up women surrounded him and deposited him on a fluffy white pillow near the entrance.

"Oh, Veronica, he's so handsome."

"I know," she said smugly.

"I can't believe you brought him here." One peered close enough to get a good look at his pores. "I can't believe he came!"

"He had no choice." Veronica fingered the ends of her hair. The locks of blond that he used to think was the most beautiful thing he'd ever seen.

Now he knew better. It was all fake. For someone who

was so into speaking the truth, he thought that was kind of ironic.

A gal in a black smock looked them up and down. "Water?"

Just as Jarred was about to accept gratefully, Veronica nodded. "Yes, please, with lemon."

And then she turned and walked away. Without a word to him. He was reduced to sitting there like a mascot for three hours as Veronica got herself dolled up. Her hair was colored and cut, her fingernails and toenails got fixed up. And she even went into some back room to get waxed.

Jarred hoped like hell that she would never, ever tell him what she'd just gotten pulled off. He really didn't want to know.

After three hours and ten minutes, he couldn't take another lavender-and-peony-scented minute. Seeking refuge, he walked outside. There, the air was fresher, but he still felt out of place. He missed Electra.

He missed walking out of Ed's Feed and Seed and seeing people he knew. He missed walking down the sidewalk to the bank and practicing the art of tipping his hat.

Bank. Hat tipping. Serena! Money!

He pulled out his cell phone and pushed number five on his speed dial. To his relief, she answered immediately. "Jarred?"

"Yep, it's me."

"Are you okay? I was sure you would be with Veronica today."

"I am. She's getting beautified right now."

"Oh." She paused. "Um, was there something you needed?"

"There was. Serena, I almost forgot—I owe you your bonus."

"That's why you called?" He knew her so well he could hear the smile in her voice. "I knew you'd pay me."

"Well, to tell you the truth, I called for another reason, too."

"Hmm? And what was that?"

"I just wanted to talk." To a friend, he silently added. To someone who wanted to talk to him.

"What about?"

"Oh, I don't know. What are you doing?"

After a pause, she laughed. "You're going to laugh. I'm making a cake."

"You're baking?"

"I know. Of the two of us, you're the one who's Betty Crocker, but I just had an urge to make a chocolate cake from scratch."

"How did it turn out?"

He could hear her opening the oven door. "Oh, shoot, Jarred. I don't think it rose! They look like two sorry chocolate pancakes. What do you think I did wrong?"

Though his body was sitting on a sunny park bench—and his eyes were on a beauty-shop door—in his mind, he was sitting next to Serena. "Pull out those cake pans and read me the recipe."

She laughed. "Really? You have time for this?"

"Sweetheart, I can honestly say, I can't think of anything I'd rather do than discuss your pitiful cake."

"All right, then."

Jarred propped one leg across the other while they talked about her cake. He smiled when she realized she'd forgotten baking powder.

Laughed when she took a taste test and groaned.

He knew he couldn't go a week without seeing her—she made him too happy, that was just how it was. "Hey, why don't you come on over tonight?" he asked.

"Tonight? Jarred, aren't you Veronica's around the clock?"

"I don't think we're going to want to spend the night together," he said drily. "I'd pretty much bet money on that."

"Are you sure?"

"I'm positive. Please say you'll stop by."

"I really shouldn't—"

Eyeing the beauty salon's door, he began to dread Veronica coming out. "When you come by, I'll give you your bonus, and we'll make a new cake together."

"I don't think so."

"Okay, how about you come over and read a little bit of Penelope to Ginny and me?"

"To you, too?"

"Heck, yeah! I'm dying to know what's happening with that poor horse."

"All right. Eight o'clock?"

"That's fine." The front door opened. "I've got to go. See you then," he said before hurriedly clicking off and coming face-to-face with a very beautiful Veronica Snow.

Glancing at his phone as though it was about to explode, she said, "Who were you talking to?"

"I don't think it's any of your business."

"It sounds like it was another woman."

He wasn't about to lie. "It was."

Her lips formed a pretty little pout. "Jarred, I'm afraid I don't understand."

When he hadn't known her…when he'd only thought of Veronica Snow as his unobtainable perfection, he would have wanted to kiss her. Tease away that pout. Now he only wished she'd pout in somebody else's direction.

'Course, that wasn't her fault. As nicely as possible, he tried to explain. "You paid for my time. You didn't say you were going to monitor everything I've been doing. Or comment on every person I talk to."

For a moment, her feelings looked hurt. Then, still staring at him, she swung her now exceptionally beautiful hair onto one shoulder. "I'm ready to go try on shoes."

"Great," he said with as much forced politeness as he could conjure up. "Are we walking or driving?"

"We can walk, I suppose."

As Serena had shown him how to do, Jarred gently pressed his fingertips to the small of Veronica's back and led her to the sidewalk. Next he held out his arm, taking care to be on the side of the road, just in case some fool driver lost control and decided to head their way.

With a grateful look, she took his arm and for good measure, stepped a little closer.

Then they started walking. More than one envious-looking man turned their way. Jarred looked them right back in the eyes, his expression full and cocky.

Yes, this scenario was just the kind of thing he'd had in mind when he'd asked Serena for help. He wanted to be seen with Veronica. He wanted to feel sharp and special when other people looked at the beautiful, classy woman on his arm.

He wanted men of all ages to wish they were him.

And, well, he'd done it.

But what he hadn't counted on was just how empty he was feeling inside. The truth of the matter was that Veronica was a lot of work. Her interests were fancy and smart and made him feel as though he hadn't traveled anywhere, hadn't gone to enough schools and always had a piece of spinach stuck between his teeth.

He didn't care for the feeling.

She cuddled closer, brushing his arm with a breast. But her compact curves didn't turn him on the way someone else's did.

And when she looked at him, he knew he should be overcome by her beauty. But as he stared at her perfectly shaped brows, all he could do was wonder what it felt like to have hair ripped from your body.

"Jarred, I'm sorry I snapped at you. I guess I was just jealous."

Remembering how much she'd paid for him, he pretended he was in Dodge City, Kansas, and partying with the rodeo sponsors. Those men had wanted to feel special and important, too. Jarred had been happy to oblige because he'd liked having money in his wallet.

It was a bit of a surprise to realize that the two situations weren't all that different. "Oh, Veronica, you have nothing to be jealous about. You're the most beautiful girl in the city. And I'm not lying. I truly believe that."

She looked bemused. "You know, I actually do believe you."

"You should. Why, if all these envious women around us had lasers in their eyes, you'd be burned to a crisp. And that would be a cryin' shame."

He held his breath. Was he laying it on too thick? Society girls like Veronica surely saw through all that malarkey quicker than most of the rodeo women population.

But she just tapped him on his forearm. "Oh, Jarred. The things you say."

"I'm sorry. I know I'm a little rough around the edges."

"But that's why I wanted you. Because you are rough. Because you're so different from most men I've dated."

Jarred didn't necessarily care for how she made him sound. "Different can be good."

"Yes, it can." Veronica looked him over slowly. "And here, we have a whole week together."

"It's going to be a helluva week, that's for sure."

"I hope so. I sure don't want to waste a minute of our time

together. Not one moment." As he was digesting that, she pointed to the door of an extremely ritzy shoe shop. "We're here."

"I suppose you want me in there with you?"

"Of course. I mean, you want to help me decide what shoes to wear for our dinner tonight, don't you?"

"Sure I do," he lied. "But it needs to be an early one, okay? I've got a few other commitments I can't ignore."

"But I paid for your time. Isn't there anyone else who can take care of those commitments for you?"

"Not a solitary soul," he murmured as he sat on a too-small chair and watched Veronica slip expensive shoes on and off.

As he did so, he remembered his mother's best advice ever: Son, be careful what you wish for…you just might get it.

Chapter Twenty

"Is Jarred not here?" Serena looked at her watch again as she stood facing Cal Jr. on the front step. "I could have sworn he told me to come over at eight o'clock."

"He's out in the barn, attending to chores. I imagine he'll be back pretty soon."

"Oh." Now she felt three times the fool. Surely there was nothing more pathetic than a woman showing up at a taken man's home. Embarrassed, she stepped away. "Well, please tell him I'll come back some other time."

"Oh, no, you don't. Go on out there and see him. He was planning on seeing you. He's not hard to miss." He winked. "He'll be the sweaty guy in the straw hat."

"Well, all right." Shifting her purse so she could carry it more easily on her shoulder, Serena walked back down the front walkway, across the driveway and then down the little pebble-filled path to the barn.

She'd never been inside. There'd been no reason to go in, of course. But close-up, it looked like something out of a fancy design magazine. State-of-the-art stalls and feeding troughs blended in with an open, fuel-efficient design. Scents of hay and wood and horse mixed in with the richer aroma of fine leather. The Riddells sure knew how to outfit a barn. The horses who lived inside had to be the luckiest horses in God's creation.

Feeling vaguely silly, she walked through the main entrance. Most likely Jarred had been exercising some of his stock.

"Hello?" she said a bit tentatively. "Hello? Jarred?"

He poked his head out of one of the stalls, his face stained with dirt and grime. When he met her gaze, he visibly winced. "Serena? Oh, shoot."

Well, that hadn't been the greeting she'd expected when she'd driven over. Moving closer, she saw he was sitting on an upturned water barrel. Next to him was a handsome colt. Knowing better than to scare the young horse, she leaned over the railing and admired him. "Oh, Jarred. He's a beauty."

"I think so. He's got incredible bloodlines—we'll get a good price for him." Reaching out, he rubbed the colt's nose. When the horse nipped at him lightly, he chuckled. "But for now, he's just a character." After another pat, he stood up. "Seri, I'm sorry you had to go hunting for me. I lost track of time."

"I didn't mind. Actually, I kind of like seeing you in here. It's been ages since we've hung out together in a barn."

"Not since 4-H." Easily, he bypassed the gate and stuck a foot through the slats. His hip followed, then finally his shoulders and head.

It wasn't anything he or she hadn't done a hundred times before. But it had been a while since Serena had seen him in this element. Sometime that afternoon, he'd stripped off his shirt. Now he only wore a thin undershirt, stained with sweat and grime.

And his jeans? Well, he wasn't wearing his usual city cowboy Wranglers. No, these were faded Levis, slim fitting, soft from dozens of washings. Frayed from years of hard work.

This was the Jarred she knew, the guy who worked hard and had no need to know about etiquette books. This was the boy with whom she'd shared burgers and barbecue on the back porch of restaurants…not the citified slicker who tried to wear designer shirts but never looked quite right.

This was the guy who still took her breath away with one slow, sexy grin. Her mouth went dry.

He noticed.

Looking down at himself, he frowned. "Shoot," he said again. "I probably smell to high heaven. I'm sorry."

And before she could tell him that, no, she really didn't mind that he wasn't all spit-polished and clean, he grabbed the edge of that ratty, soiled undershirt and pulled it over his head.

Revealing a bronzed chest full of muscles over a six-pack of toned abs. And every bit of that skin was as smooth as silk.

Only then did she notice that he was unbuttoning his jeans. Right there in front of her. "Jarred, what are you doing?"

He looked at her as if she was crazy. "I'm going to wash up."

"Here?"

"No, in the bathroom down the hall. There's a shower." Before he turned, he looked her way again. "What's wrong?"

"Nothing." For a second, she tried really hard not to stare at the fine line of dark hair that ran down his stomach. But it was a futile thing. "I mean, it's just, well… You're gorgeous."

He laughed. "Seri, I didn't think you noticed."

Oh, wasn't that trademark Jarred? No modesty. No embarrassment that his shirt was off and his jeans were only staying up by a prayer. She tried to laugh, too. But instead of sounding merry, it just sounded strained and kind of restless.

Then there was only one thing to say. "I noticed. I've always noticed."

There. Her silly, childish crush was out in the open. Now

he could roll his eyes and put some much-needed space in between them.

Biting her lip, she waited one second. Two. Waited for him to laugh her words off. Or worse, get embarrassed for her.

But instead of doing any of that, he stepped a little closer and ran one finger over her lip. "You do that a lot," he murmured. "You bite your bottom lip."

It took everything she had to stand still. "It's a habit."

"Yeah?" Interest sparked his eyes as he dropped his hand. "I happen to have a few of my own." He stepped a little closer, close enough for her to spread her legs a bit to accommodate his size. Close enough for the unbuttoned waistband of his jeans to brush against her shirt.

"What habits do you have?"

"I look at you too much. I think about your long legs." He reached out and curved his palms over her hips, their heat branding her. "I think about holding you close like this with no clothes on." He lowered his voice. "I think about kissing you night and day…"

Her hands went to his shoulders. "You do?" she whispered.

"Uh-huh." He leaned closer. "Night and day," he repeated softly, then he slid his hands around her backside and finally brushed her lips with his.

Years of restraint and proper behavior collapsed in a heartbeat. When their lips met again, Serena leaned closer hungrily. She tilted her head, opened for his tongue, felt his teeth knock against hers as he complied.

Oh, he tasted so good! Like hot summer days and the thick, tantalizing heat of July. He tasted like Jarred. And he kissed like a dream.

His hands reached higher, pulled off the elastic binding her hair. As her hair fell down her back, Jarred kissed her again, slower this time, nibbling her bottom lip, traipsing his lips across her cheek. Making her nerve endings practically scream.

She sighed.

He pulled away. Fingers still tangled in her hair, he looked at her square in the eye. "I like you, Serena."

"I like you, too."

He slid one hand down her spine. "I care for you and I think you're lovely."

That embarrassed her. She wasn't anything special. "Jar—"

He kissed her again. Cutting off her response, tenderly deepening the kiss until she could hardly think straight, let alone talk.

And that was just as well because he seemed to have plenty to say. "I think you're gorgeous. I love your legs. I love your pretty green eyes. I even love the way you give me what-for. But most of all, right this minute, I really love the way you're looking at me—like you want me, too."

"I do," she said simply.

Pure pleasure lit his eyes as he grabbed her arm and pulled her into a short hallway. Then, before she even had a chance to ask him where he was headed, he pulled her into what had to be the fanciest barn bathroom in the whole state of Texas.

And locked the door. Reached in the clear glass enclosure and turned on not one but two showerheads. And then reached for her again.

Steam filled the room as he kissed her breathless once more. A slow, sexy smile made her insides melt as he unbuttoned the rest of that fly and pulled his jeans down, somehow using the bootjack and pulling off his boots along the way.

Now clad only in a pair of black knit boxers, Jarred Riddell was surely every girl's dream come true.

"You're going to shower?" she asked idiotically.

"Uh-huh," he murmured, reaching for her. "'Course, you

are, too." Nimble fingers untucked her T-shirt and pulled it over her head. Two seconds later, her bra hit the tile floor.

With great care, he reached out and cupped one of her breasts. As he ran a thumb over a nipple, he smiled. "Lord have mercy, Serena. You are a sight. Come get wet with me."

She stood there, more than a little bit stunned by the chain of events as he slid his boxers off and walked into the shower. The glass door closed again as he stood under the spray.

As she unbuttoned her own jeans, she saw her reflection in the mirror. She'd never been a particularly shy girl, but the sight of herself, bare breasted, flushed from the steam, glowing from his kisses—well, it was a bit unsettling.

"Serena, you need some help, darlin'?"

"I got it."

He opened the shower door and peeked out. "Can you get your boots off?"

She slid a heel in the jack and pulled. "I can."

Then, she couldn't believe it, but there he stood, shower door open, spray spattering out, steam sliding upward and slick as an otter. Watching her slide her jeans down.

When she turned to toss them on the counter, he moaned low. "Never imagined you were a thong girl, Seri."

There was little to do now but push the scrap of lace down her thighs. "Is that a good thing? Or—"

Before she could finish the question, he snaked out a hand and yanked her inside. Hot water showered over her as he brought his lips to her own.

Eagerly, she pressed against him, tasting mint and Jarred.

His hands ran the length of her, getting to know her in the most intimate of ways. She ran her hands along his shoulders, moaned when his lips found the nape of her neck. And still the hot water rained down on them.

Now this was something she'd never imagined. Not even in her most vivid dreams.

But something in her reaction must have caused a thread of doubt. A wariness. Shifting them again so the water was only skimming off her shoulders, he gently lifted her chin. "I just realized I'm taking things a little fast. Are you okay?"

"With shower sex in a barn?" She almost smiled. "I'm okay."

But he didn't kiss her again. Instead, he carefully rearranged a handful of wet hair that had fallen over her shoulder.

"Serena, honey…this isn't your first time, is it?"

"No…"

Instead of looking relieved, he tilted his head. As if he knew there was more to the story. "But…?"

"But I haven't done this a whole lot."

He waited a beat. "Once?"

"Twice. And, um, never in a shower." As a little bit of the light fell from his eyes, her heart sank. Please don't stop, she entreated silently. *Please don't make me wonder what being with you would be like….*

He reached behind him and turned off the water.

Immediately, she chilled. "Jarred, I don't want to stop."

"I don't want to, either," he replied softly, his voice a little tender, a little more strained. "It just, uh, occurred to me that I don't have any protection in here. And, um, well, I don't want to shock you by doing all kinds of things to you on the wall of a shower stall."

Towels materialized out of nowhere. He wrapped her in one, then wrapped another around his hips.

Before she could ask where he *did* want to do all those things, he grabbed her hand and led her out of the bathroom, down the hall and into the office. Gently pushing her to the couch, he murmured, "Sit." She pulled up her towel as he reached in a drawer, fished around and pulled out a packet.

And then, before she could even think to ask if what they were doing was right, before she could get chilled or even wonder why in the world he stowed condoms in his desk drawer, Jarred leaned close and claimed her lips again.

And then it was the most logical thing in the world to slip out of her towel and wrap her arms around him again. Feeling the heat of his skin, running her hands along the muscles of his back. Before she knew it, Jarred was lying on top of her, pushing her hair off her face, kissing her neck. Nudging her legs apart, covering himself, touching her, caressing her, murmuring sweet things.

Making love to her.

Serena wrapped her legs around him and held him close. Making love with Jarred was wonderful. Sweet. She had imagined it might be awkward, but it wasn't. She'd thought she would feel self-conscious. She didn't.

Instead, she savored each touch. The thrust of his hips. The way he coaxed her. Praised her. All too soon, they found release. She arched her back in pleasure, and hugged him tight when he did the same.

When they caught their breaths, Jarred gathered her close in his arms and kissed her again. "I'm so glad we did that."

She looked into his eyes. He was such a handsome man. Such a good man, too. "I am, too," she said. And she knew that whatever happened, she had spoken the truth.

For just a little while, she had been the only thing Jarred Riddell had been thinking about. The only woman on his mind.

He brushed his lips against her brow, her cheek. "I can't explain it, but being with you is so perfect, you know?"

"You really think so?" Hope lifted her. Made her imagine a thousand days in his company, a thousand nights in his arms. Maybe everything would work out between them after all.

Then she could look back on her years of infatuation with a fondness instead of as a multitude of wasted opportunities.

"I guess that's because we've been friends for so long."

"We sure have been," she agreed.

His gaze warmed, and then he closed his eyes and kissed her again, lingering over her lips, making her heart melt. Making her imagine a lifetime of dreams…a lifetime of being together.

When he looked at her again, his eyes had turned a darker blue. "Yep," he said around a sigh. "What we've got is just right. We're friends, with benefits."

With one sentence, she fell back down to earth. "Excuse me?"

Picking up a piece of straw that had found its way onto the couch, he popped it in his mouth, chewing it like a toothpick. "Well, I'm just saying that I doubt things will ever be this comfortable with me and anyone else."

Will ever be? With anyone else? She was dreaming about fairy-tale happy endings while Jarred was dreaming about hookups with other women?

Dammit!

Serena's mouth went dry as once again, she cursed herself for being such a fool where Jarred Riddell was concerned.

Pulling away, Serena grabbed her towel and stalked back to the monster bathroom.

After a moment of silence, she heard Jarred scramble to his feet and trot off after her. "Seri?"

Thank the good Lord she found her underwear right away. After slipping on her thong and her bra, she glared. "Jarred Riddell, are you really talking about having sex with other women just moments after bedding me…on a barn couch?"

"No."

He looked so puzzled, so confused, her temper snapped. "Can't you at least put some clothes on?"

Shifting his weight, he folded his arms over his chest, still as naked as the day he was born. "A little while ago I was gorgeous."

Oh, when would she ever learn?

Turning from him, she grabbed her shirt and covered herself. She'd just stuck one foot in her jeans when he spoke. "Serena, what's wrong?"

"Everything. We shouldn't have done this." After buttoning her jeans, she pulled on a boot.

Behind her, she could hear him finally getting dressed, too. "I wasn't lying. I do like you, Serena."

"I know." Even to her own ears, her words sounded deflated. Or, maybe it was that she finally was getting smarter where he was concerned.

Though her eyes stung, Serena felt almost as though she was turning over a new leaf, right then and there. Because, well…there was friendship. And there was an unfortunate crush. But there was pride, too.

It was about time she found hers. With as much grace as she could, she slipped on her other boot.

Jarred watched her. "Will an apology even help? I really do care for you, honey. And what we shared, it was great." He wrinkled his nose. "It was better than that. I promise."

She shrugged. "Jarred, I'm not going to pretend that what we did wasn't wonderful. But, maybe it's time we both realized that it's time to move on. See, the thing of it is…where you're concerned…you've always kind of been my Achilles' heel. There's been pretty much nothing that I wouldn't do for you. But it's time I stopped that, don't you think?"

Without waiting for an answer, unable to even guess what he was thinking, she started walking.

"Serena, honey, let's talk—"

"There's nothing left to say." One pull of the door handle brought a welcome escape. Though Serena heard Jarred

fussing behind her again—pulling on his boots, most likely—
she forced herself to keep walking.

Yes, that's what she needed to do. Just walk away. Walk
away from the lessons and the stupid, silly crush.

Grow up.

And realize that Jarred Riddell was never going to be hers.
Not in the way she'd dreamed about, at least. It was time she
came to terms with that.

"Serena? Dammit. Wait!"

She was outside now, almost at her car.

"Seri? What the heck do you want?"

She wanted the whole shebang—love, marriage, babies.
But she knew Jarred couldn't give her those things.

That, of course, was why leaving was so easy.

After everything they'd shared, she would have thought
it would have been extremely painful to leave without even
looking back.

But, actually, it wasn't difficult to do at all.

Chapter Twenty-One

It had been a long and tiring week. After futilely trying to call Serena and talk to her time and again, Jarred decided to table their problems until he was done fussing with Veronica. They only had one more scheduled date until he fulfilled his auction requirements.

Though part of him chafed at the idea of letting even more time pass before he patched things up with Serena, the part with a brain figured it was probably good to have some time to iron things out.

Fact was, he was confused. For pretty much most of his life, he'd always taken Serena's friendship for granted. It had lain in the back of his mind like an old present. He'd appreciated her friendship, but he hadn't pulled it out and examined it for a while.

Now that they'd done their lessons and he'd gotten to know her again…Jarred knew he was falling in love with her. Their little escapade in the barn had been a sweet bonus. Their intimacy had clinched it. What they had was special.

Then, somehow, he'd managed to mess things up. Much of the time since they'd parted, he'd spent hours remembering every minute they'd had together, making love. Trying to figure out what had happened. Had he been too rough? Had he shocked her?

But instinctively, he'd known that hadn't been it. Of course, it had been something he'd said. But what? Had she wanted professions of love while he'd said "like"?

Had she wanted promises when he hadn't made any? Those were logical choices, but somehow that didn't seem right, either.

He ended up just mailing her a check for her thousand-dollar bonus and calling it a day.

But finally it was Saturday and he and Veronica were half-way through their very last date. After going to Veronica's door, she'd kept him waiting almost a half hour while she primped.

Then when she appeared, she spent another thirty minutes discussing her clothing and hair problems. Then he heard about her mother's troubles.

He felt sorry for that. He felt sorry for both Midge and Veronica. But after another long tirade about the nursing staff and other frustrations, Jarred knew that he couldn't take another evening like this again.

Then, just as they were walking to his Corvette, she delivered a whale of a question. "Jarred, just where do you see the two of us going?"

"In the future?"

"Of course. How do you want to take things next week?"

He didn't want to take her anywhere. "Well…about that."

"Just tell me how you feel."

Oh, this was going to be bad. He'd kind of hoped they could drift apart after this evening's date, but now—in the mother of all ironies—he was going to have to break things off with her. "Actually, I don't think we're meant for each other."

"You don't?"

"No. Truth is, I don't think we suit." He braced himself for a litany of insults. Of professions that he'd broken her heart. But instead of looking mad as hell and irritated, she looked… reflective. "What do you think about that?"

Slowly, she smiled. "I was actually thinking the same thing." Placing a hand on his arm, she said, "Don't get me wrong, I do like you. More than I thought I would. But, well, we're pretty different, wouldn't you say?"

Heck, they were as different as peas and peanut butter. "I would." He pulled on his shirt collar. "Veronica, since I'm telling truths like nobody's business, it's probably time for a full disclosure. Fact is, I'm not who you think I am. Fact is, I've been living a lie."

"What? Jarred, what are you talking about?"

"See, that's what I'm talking about. I shouldn't even be going to dinner parties. I'm not the kind of guy who wears suits like this and does fancy stuff. Ever."

"But you acted like it would be fun."

"Only because you paid me to be with you."

Shock splashed red on her face. "Only?"

He brushed a hand over his face. "I'm sorry. See, this is a prime example of what I've been trying to tell you. I'm no good. Fact is, I'm just as rude and crude and obnoxious as any other cowboy you've ever met. Probably worse than most."

"No. You've been great. You have perfect manners…."

Feeling as if he'd taken truth serum, he started spilling his guts. "Well. Um. There's a story to all that. It all started the first time I saw you. I thought you were beautiful."

She rolled her eyes. "Enough about—"

"It's true. I thought you were the prettiest thing I'd ever seen in my life. I wanted to get to know you. But the only way I could think to ever get some time with you was that auction. So I paid Serena Higgens to help."

"To help how?"

"I paid her to help me become the man I thought you would like. She taught me how to open doors and use the right forks. She taught me to be good enough for you."

A moment passed. Finally, she said, "I've seen the way Serena looks at you."

"That's the thing. While we were together, I started realizing that she's the person I need. We're better suited. I'm rough and tumble and have serious difficulties with double negatives. She's okay with that. I never meant for my feelings to change."

For a full five minutes, they sat in silence. Then she surprised him. "You know, I can understand what you're saying. We don't have control over our hearts, I don't think. Things just happen."

"Do you really think love is like that?"

A sad little smile lit her face. "I do."

"What do you want to do about the dinner party?"

She chuckled. "You'd really still go with me?"

"I promised I would."

Lifting a hand, she caressed his cheek. "You know what? I think you would. But if you don't mind, I'd much rather go on my own. I think I'm going to tell everyone I've had enough of my rough-around-the-edges cowboy."

"Are you sure?" He felt like the biggest heel imaginable. "You paid a lot of money…"

"Oh, don't kid yourself, Jarred. You're a good man. But that money was for charity. For orphans, remember?"

"I'm so grateful you're not tarring and feathering me, I think I'll give them a sizable donation myself."

Veronica grinned. "See? Everything always works out for the best…sooner or later."

When his dad took a turn for the worse late that night, Jarred hoped Veronica's advice was the truth.

Chapter Twenty-Two

When his dad had started experiencing chest pains late at night, Jarred had called Serena from the hospital.

"I know I shouldn't be callin' you, but I need a friend right now," he'd said.

And with those words, all the hurt she'd been storing inside her faded away. She would always be his friend. "What's wrong?"

"Dad had another attack. It's bad, Seri."

Instantly, she'd offered to help out with Virginia. Even though Gwen had said she'd be fine with sleeping over for a few days, Serena wanted to help out as much as she could.

"Can you go to the house soon?" he'd asked.

"Of course." She'd arrived only moments after everyone but Virginia and Gwen had gone to the hospital.

After visiting with Gwen a bit and saying goodbye, Serena checked up on the little girl. Ginny was sound asleep, so she'd settled in the guest room, then had done her best the following morning to ease Virginia's worries.

Things with Cal Sr. had been iffy for a time. But finally his condition had stabilized and they'd brought him back home.

After that, she'd visited quite a bit. The adults in the house were tired, and Virginia seemed to enjoy being with her. Serena felt the same way.

Now, three days later, they were back at the ranch and

sitting on the couch together. Over a tall glass of iced tea Serena found herself eyeing Jarred carefully and hoping things would settle down for the Riddells soon. Jarred looked plain exhausted.

"How's your father doing today?" she asked.

After a good long pause, Jarred answered. "He's not doing so good today, if you want to know the truth. He's about the color of a bedsheet at the end of a season. Kind of gray."

Worried about the lines that looked determined to settle in Jarred's brow permanently, Serena scooted forward in her chair. "What can I do to help?"

"Not a thing. You've already helped a lot. I don't know what we would have done if you hadn't been here to help us out with Virginia."

"I enjoyed being with her."

"She likes you. We all do." His gaze flickered across her face, across her lips, and softened with something that looked like love. "But I'm sure you've got other things to do."

That was the problem. At the moment, nothing sounded as important or as dear to her as staying there. "I can't think of anything else. Since Hannah is working at the library tonight, I've got nothing but time on my hands. Do you mind if I stay here a little longer? Penelope is up to her ears in trouble again."

Jarred smiled. "That horse is a menace to society. She's really accident-prone for a Tennessee walker."

She played along with the silly conversation. "I heard that breed is like that. Nothing but trouble. So, you don't mind if I stay for a while?"

"Of course not. I'd love your company." His eyes flickered over hers. "You wouldn't mind?"

"I don't mind."

"Then please stay. I need you."

The air between them stilled. Her mouth went dry.

As she looked into his eyes, at his need…and felt her own yearnings for him surface as well, everything else in the room faded away.

When Jarred stepped closer and linked his fingers through hers, her pulse jumped a bit. So did her mind. Now all she could think about was wrapping herself around him again.

Which was a very, very bad idea.

Squeezing her hand, he murmured, "So…do you want to go outside?"

It was hot out. The temperature was most likely hovering in the eighties. Fireflies and crickets and frogs were out in abundance, too. So was the humidity.

But as usual, none of that seemed to deter her from what she wanted most—to be in his company. "Sure."

It seemed only natural to take his hand and she followed him outside to the back porch.

Still holding his hand, she walked to the edge of the patio and looked out. Breathing deeply, she smelled the earth. Smelled the fresh-cut hay and the faint scent of horses and felt the heat radiating from the ground.

She leaned a little closer to him. "It's awfully nice out here."

"Yes, ma'am."

They stared at each other. A hundred promises, mixed in with almost as many regrets, hung unanswered in the air. "Serena, you've been a good friend to me. You've helped me in all kinds of ways over the years."

"You've been a good friend, too."

"Can we ever get back to normal?"

She didn't know how they could. She wasn't sure what was normal with Jarred anymore. Was it teaching him how to be with another woman?

Accepting his help when a certain banker got a little too fresh?

Was it normal kissing him in a barn? Doing so much more?

Tension filled his eyes as he searched her face. "Serena, are you ever gonna tell me what I did wrong?"

She sighed. "Jarred—"

"When we were together, did I do something wrong? Do you have regrets—"

"You didn't do anything wrong." Well, besides saying all the wrong things, she supposed. But maybe all that wasn't his fault. Maybe it was more like hers. After all, he'd never promised her anything. She'd been the one imagining they could go from friends to lovers easily. "It has more to do with me than anything."

"What do you mean?"

She bit her lip. "Can we not talk about it just yet?"

"Don't you think we should?"

"Not right now." Talking about things would only make things awkward between them. She'd embarrass him with her dreams of a future and he'd say all the wrong things again.

"You know I'm going to bring it up again."

"Maybe next time you do, I'll feel like talking."

"Hope so." Slowly, he wrapped his arms around her, loosely holding her in front of him. Because she was in no mood to fight the wonderful feelings he gave her, she relaxed against him. Letting her shoulders rest against his chest. As always, her body seemed to fit just right next to his.

When she leaned her head back against him, he adjusted his hands, linking his fingers low across her hips. His scent surrounded her, drawing her closer to him, making her let her guard down.

She sighed. "This is nice."

"It is. I'm glad we came out here."

His lips were on her neck. Messing with her mind.

Though she knew no good would come of it, she turned in his arms and looped her hands around his neck. His blue eyes danced. Then he lowered his head and kissed her once again. Wrapped his arms around her and held her close.

Serena kissed him right back, meeting his lips, opening her mouth so he could gain entrance. Jarred curved his arms around her middle and stepped closer. And the kiss deepened.

Only when she needed air did they separate.

But when she looked into his eyes, it was obvious nothing had changed. Jarred Riddell liked kissing her, that was true.

But really, there was nothing else there.

Oh, she needed to get away from him. "You know what, I think I'll go now."

"Now what's wrong?"

There was so much tension and irritation in his voice, she finally snapped. "What's wrong, Jarred, is nothing new. What's wrong is I'm in love with you."

"Huh?"

"Come on. Do you really think I would have slept with you just because we're friends?"

He coughed. "Serena, listen. I care for you, I do."

"Oh, I know, Jarred." Moments passed. After he said nothing else, just looked at her, all confused and miserable, she nodded. "All right, then. I think I had better get going."

"Serena, listen, maybe we could talk some more—"

"I think we've probably talked enough. Actually, let's not talk for a while, okay?"

She left him standing there in the dark.

She hoped she'd know better than to ever stop by again. A girl could only take so much.

Chapter Twenty-Three

As Serena sped down the expansive Riddell driveway, she knew she was in a heap of trouble. What had she been thinking? Making out with him on his back porch.

He wasn't hers.

Furthermore, she'd made sure of it!

She was thinking about things she shouldn't be thinking of. Imagining a future with Jarred that had nothing to do with simple friendship and everything to do with waking up next to him every morning.

Being over at Jarred's home, being in his arms, it was magic. Voodoo magic. After kissing him, then kissing him again, she'd been ready to do just about anything he'd wanted.

Shoot. She hadn't been sitting around waiting for him to make the moves; no, she'd had an agenda all her own. And it sure hadn't been something her mother would have been proud of. Because basically, she would have taken off every stitch of clothing she'd had on with just a little bit more encouragement. Things between them had been that good.

And that was bad.

She didn't often speed around Electra, but at the moment, driving her Corolla at the speed limit had no appeal. She took curves a little too fast, and sped down the hills faster than she ever had in her life.

Around her, woods filled with pine trees and oaks stood sentry in the evening.

She put her windows down and felt the breeze blow back her hair. Smelled the earth. Felt free.

Oh, it felt so good to be reckless! That, of course, was something she never was.

That little statement was a joke if she ever heard one. She'd been reckless with Jarred. She'd allowed her feelings to take control. And then she'd done everything she could to push him toward somebody else.

Someone who would never truly appreciate him like she did. In front of her, the road narrowed and began a slow incline. She was nearing the entrance to the town.

Her heart rate slowed along with her speed.

And as she was returning to reality a pair of deer popped out of the woods and leaped toward the road.

She swerved and slammed her foot on the brake.

Just in time to meet the second animal head-on.

Her windshield cracked as she screeched to a stop, then slid into a ditch.

When she came to, Paula McCall was peering close, her expression a sea of worry. "Serena? Serena, are you okay? I was driving the other way when I saw those deer come out of nowhere! Oh, my goodness! Look at your windshield! I think that deer's rack broke right through!"

Bleary, she opened an eye and tried not to cry in pain.

Paula pulled out her cell phone. "I'm going to call an ambulance. Don't move."

That advice wasn't hard to follow. As Paula talked on the phone, Serena moved her arms and legs. Nothing felt broken but her body felt beaten up. As much as she dared, she opened the other eye. "Thanks for stopping."

"No problem. They're sending someone out right now. We'll take you in to the urgent care to be on the safe side."

Her surroundings flashed and swirled. Oh, she was about to lose consciousness. Shooting pains shot through her leg and zipped directly to her brain. Before everything went black, she muttered, "Paula, I'm just going to rest for a bit."

In the vague recesses of her brain, through the dense fog, she heard Paula's reply. "Hang in there, honey. Help is on the way."

"What's wrong with her?"

Junior curled one large hand around his arm. "I'm not sure, but I heard it's nothing too serious. She's bruised and beat up. Maybe a concussion?"

It all sounded serious to him. "Dammit. She should have called me. I would have taken her here."

"I think Paula found her. Settle down, now. Serena's going to be fine."

Jarred's temper flared. "I'll settle down after I see her." Looking at his watch, he said, "A whole hour's gone by. Why do you think they haven't come out to tell us what's going on?"

His brother shoved him into an uncomfortable plastic seat. As Jarred sat with a thump, Junior stepped in front of him. "You've got to lower your voice and stop carrying on. If you don't, all you're going to be seeing is the front door of this place."

Unclenching his hands, Jarred nodded. "I hear you."

"Good."

Antsy and still worried sick, he fought to think of something else. "So, do you know about Serena's car?"

"I know it's totaled. But cars can be fixed. And Serena's getting fixed up, too."

The peaceful, almost zen tone in his brother's voice irked him like nothing other. Jarred jumped to his feet and jerked away from Junior's restraining hand. "I'm fine. Don't grab me again."

"Then act fine. What has gotten into you? I know you like Serena, we all like her. But it's not like she's your girlfriend…"

"She might be."

"Might?" Junior gave Trent a none-too-subtle look of exasperation. "What happened to Veronica?"

"You know what happened. We didn't suit."

"And now, after all this time, you've decided you and Serena do?" Trent asked.

"It's not like that. I've had feelings for her for a while."

But instead of being cowed by his tone, Junior folded his arms over his chest. "Shoot. We all knew that."

Maybe pride was overrated. "Y'all did?"

"She's always been yours…at least from where Trent and I've been sitting."

"We've been buddies."

"And more." Junior cleared his throat. "Have you told her?"

"What?"

"That you love her?"

"Not in so many words." Why hadn't he? Was he so afraid of falling in love that he was willing to jeopardize everything he had with her?

Junior bent his head down. "You know, just because Dad had bad luck with women doesn't mean you will."

"Dad didn't have bad luck…" But even as he said the words, Jarred knew that had been the heart of the problem. The best woman in the world—his mother—had left them too early. And then his father's second wife had taken off, too.

And he, being the oldest, had decided the only way to keep his heart in check was to not give it away.

So, he'd fooled around with women who didn't mean much.

And he'd yearned for a beautiful girl who seemed pretty much unreachable.

And he'd kept the person who he'd fallen in love with nearby, but not too close. In case something happened to her. So he wouldn't get hurt again.

But in spite of his best intentions, the worst had happened anyway. She'd gotten hurt…and he was only now realizing that she'd had his heart for some time. Maybe for most of his life.

He'd just been too scared to acknowledge it.

Yep, the truth was as obvious as a cow with colic. He was completely, totally in love with Serena.

"Let's go talk to the nurse," he murmured. "I can't stand around and wait any longer."

"I'll follow you."

Surprised by the easy acquiescence he heard in his brother's voice, Jarred nodded his thanks. Junior had never been one to easily boss around. He might be younger, but he had Jarred by a good fifty pounds, and he'd been a state qualifier in wrestling. No one but a fool picked a fight with him.

Luckily, the nurse was Rachel Williams. She'd gone to school with all of them. "Hey, Rach, when can I see Serena?"

"Not for a while, I'm afraid. It's supposed to be only family right now."

"Who's with her?"

Rachel frowned. "Unfortunately, nobody. Her sister is at some convention in Dallas, and her parents are in Oklahoma. She's alone."

"So let me in."

As if she was passing him notes in English class back when they were sophomores, she looked to her right and left, then gave him a little nod. "All right. She's due to be out soon anyway. The doctor just finished patching her up."

"Then she can go home?"

A small smile played on the corners of her mouth. "Yes. Well, as soon as someone can take her home."

"I can do that."

"I'll write that down. But we should probably check with Serena, too." She stopped outside a room. "The doctor's supposed to be in to see her again soon. Don't rile her up."

He turned the door handle before she'd taken three steps away.

Chapter Twenty-Four

Serena's body hurt like crazy. She had about a dozen cuts and a whole lot of bruises. And two fractured ribs.

But all that was nothing compared to the way her heart skipped a beat when Jarred entered the room.

"Hey, honey," he murmured as he walked to where she was sitting. "It looks like that deer got the best of you."

"I've never liked you hunting them, but this one, he's all yours."

"I'll grab him from the side of the road and put his head on my wall," he said with a smile. "We'll hang hats on the antlers. How's that?"

She tried to smile, but a pulsating pain nearly blinded her. "Good."

His smile faltered. "We'll get you out of here soon so you can rest."

"You don't need to do that…I know you've got your dad to think about."

"There's four of us for him. I'd rather concentrate on you."

He reached out to her again, clicking his tongue as he found a bruise on her arm, and a mess of scrapes on her bare foot. "Oh, honey."

Everything in her wanted to believe that he was there because he really cared. Well, more than as just friends. But too many times she'd fooled herself into thinking that there was something special between them when there wasn't. "Why are you here?"

Gently, he pressed his lips to her brow. "You know why. I'm here because I couldn't stay away."

There was that light in his eyes that usually signaled trouble. But today it just made her feel happy. "I'm glad."

Still standing, his right hand hovered over her. "Look at that shiner on your eye. And your hands. You're all cut up."

When he still looked ready to pick her up, she lifted her hands. "I'm okay. I don't hurt too bad."

He carefully pressed both of his hands around hers. "I was thinking I could take you home. What do you think about that?"

"I don't want to be trouble."

"You won't be. I thought I'd come to your place. I'll sit with you there."

"You sure that's what you want to do?" With effort, she tried to sound casual. As though it didn't mean all that much to her if he stayed or went.

"I've never been more sure. Serena, when Gwen called me, I nearly broke the sound barrier getting here. I want to be here for you. I want you to know that absolutely."

"Thanks," she said simply. Funny how that word told so little about her true feelings. Because in reality, there was nothing more she would love than being next to him. Knowing he cared.

She liked being near him. Jarred made her feel strong and special. And, well, she had nothing to lose anymore. Maybe he was going to be Veronica's man forever. Maybe even for a short while.

He might never be hers. But there was no reason to hide her feelings any longer. She'd given herself to him—that said it all.

So, her feelings were secure, and she had to be all right with that. She may never have Jarred Riddell, but she knew he was her friend. And, well, after all those charm-school lessons, they now had a practically inseparable bond between them.

As if on cue, Dr. Warren came in. "Hi, there, Jarred. Paying a call on Serena, hmm?"

"Guess nothing gets by you."

"Nothing worthwhile," he said as he took Jarred's place by the side of her bed and pulled out a tiny light. After examining her pupils, her blood pressure, pulse and bandages, he turned to Jarred. "Serena's going to be fine, but she's going to need a few days' rest to recover completely."

"I'll make sure of that."

She waved a hand, peeved they were talking over her. "Excuse me, gentlemen, but I can't rest for a few days. I have bills to pay."

"You can work all you want," Dr. Warren said with a nod. "Next week. This week, you're taking it easy." He eyed Jarred. "Are you up to playing nurse?"

That infamous spark in his eyes flashed. "Always."

The doctor chuckled. "I'm serious, now. She's going to need some watching."

"I'll be by her side. I'm going to take her to her place and sit with her."

"Jarred—"

He placed a finger on her lips, gently hushing her. "The decision's been made, Seri. Deal with it."

Dr. Warren smiled. "Glad y'all are working things out." He handed a set of papers to Jarred. "Here are some instructions for you. Main thing is to wake her up often and keep a close eye on her. Okay?"

"I'll do that."

"Good. Now, you tell your father to take good care of himself, too. You hear?"

"Yes, sir."

Dr. Warren turned to Serena. "Call if you need anything, dear."

"I will. Thank you."

An hour later, he and Cal Jr. were walking on either side of her while one of the nurses pushed her wheelchair.

She would've thought more about it, about how she felt about things, if the blinding sun hadn't brought about a stream of unrelenting pain. She closed her eyes and hoped the pain relievers would kick in soon.

And then she fell asleep.

AFTER JUNIOR UNLOCKED her door and pushed it open, Jarred carried Serena over the threshold and into the smallest little bedroom he'd ever seen.

Serena moaned a bit in his arms. "Shh, now." Gently, he set her on the side of her bed, and clumsily pulled the pink sheets down around her. Then he helped her lie down.

She relaxed against the pillows with a heartfelt sigh.

"Sorry," she mumbled. "I'll be better soon."

"I know."

He stood there, just looking at her for another moment before returning to Junior in the kitchenette.

Junior looked at the tiny couch doubtfully. "You going to be okay bedding down here?"

"Of course. I've slept in worse places."

"We all have, but this place is tiny." Cocking an eyebrow, he added, "It looks a whole lot like a Barbie playhouse. We should have brought her home."

"You know what things are like at home. Either Dad would wake her up or Ginny would shove books her way. This is where she's comfortable. It's not all about me, you know."

"Since when?" Junior chuckled when Jarred glared. "Hey, don't get mad. You know I'm just joshing you. Listen, I'm going to get going. Call home later, you hear? One of us will bring you some food or something."

"Will do."

As soon as Junior left, Jarred moseyed around, laying his wallet and his cell phone on the kitchen counter. Next, he pulled off his boots and untucked his T-shirt.

Then he took inventory. He found some iced-tea mix and made a pitcher of that. Located a couple of cans of soup and some saltines and set the fixings on the counter.

Her bare cupboards nearly broke his heart.

Then he took a tour around her place and noticed just how limited her life had been. There weren't a lot of frills anywhere.

With a sigh, he sat down on her sofa and turned on the television. He flipped around, which took two minutes because she had something like twelve TV stations.

Finally concentrating on Dr. Phil and one woman's search for her identity, he settled in for the long haul.

She called out to him two hours later.

Chapter Twenty-Five

"Jarred?" Serena called out, her mind still fuzzy. As she looked around her dimly lit bedroom, she wondered if she'd dreamed he was at her place. Surely he had other things to do than play nursemaid?

Then, there he was, looking rumpled and, oh, ordinary. Looking as he always had. Except there was a new line of worry in between his brows.

"Seri? You okay?"

"Yeah. I mean, I think I am." Still in a fog, Serena watched him cross the room, then settle right next to her on the mattress, his hip touching her thigh. "I guess I was just seeing if you were still here. And…you are."

"I am." He brushed the hair from her brow. "You're stuck with me, sugar. I'm not going anywhere."

Something about that statement made her look at him closer. Maybe it was the husky edge to his voice. Maybe it was the spark of awareness in his eyes. But whatever it was, it sure seemed like Jarred was talking about so much more than just one evening's care.

Gosh, it sounded like he was talking about a lifetime.

While she was stewing on that, he had taken a hold of her hand and linked his fingers through hers.

"Guess what, sugar? I looked through all the paperwork

we brought with us from the hospital. You can have a bath if you want it."

"Really?" Only Jarred would know how happy that would make her feel. She took a bath every night.

"Really and truly. What do you say?"

Though her apartment was tiny, she did have the most beautiful antique bathtub. It would be heaven to have a soak. But at the moment, even sitting up seemed like too much work. "I better not," she said with regret. "I wouldn't be able to manage it."

"Why not?"

As she sat up, she had to wait a moment for her world to regain focus. "Look at me. I can hardly keep my balance as it is. Stepping in and out of a tub is going to be next to impossible."

"Heck, a little thing like that shouldn't stop you. I can help you get in and out."

"While I'm naked?" A sudden vision of him holding her tightly next to him flashed in her mind. "No, thank you."

Those blue eyes of his turned just a bit dark and languid. "Serena Higgens, after everything we did in that shower, are you turning shy on me?"

"No. And…I'm not shy. I just don't feel like getting undressed in front of you." *Anymore.*

Jarred rolled his eyes. "Now you're just being silly. Don't make this into something more than it is."

Well, that was what she was good at doing, wasn't she? Making things between them more special than they were. "Still, I'll pass."

Ignoring her, Jarred marched into her bathroom and started running the tub. Seconds later, he trotted back her way and held out his hands. "Come on, now. I'm not gonna take no for an answer, neither."

"Either," she said wearily.

He waved a hand. "Whatever. The water's hot. I poured all kinds of pink bubble bath in, and you're going to feel a lot better after you soak."

"Jarred—"

Looking almost motherly, he directed a no-nonsense stare her way. "Come on, now. Water's getting cold. As soon as you're in the water we'll cover you up in bubbles. I bet I'll hardly see a thing."

It was the "hardly" part that worried her. But still...the bath did sound awfully good...and he was being so sweet. "All right."

"It's about time," he murmured as he helped her to her feet and to walk the short distance to the bathroom. Once they were by the tub, he turned off the water and deposited her on a stool. Then he turned his back. "See how good I'm being? I'm not even trying to sneak a peek when you don't want me to. You get undressed and then I'll help you in."

Seeing his broad back made her feel a tiny bit embarrassed. Jarred was right. She was making way too big a deal about being around him with her clothes off. "All right. But don't turn around until I say so."

"Unbutton, Seri." Only Jarred could sound so exasperated while he was doing her a favor.

"Hold on a sec."

Now that she wasn't feeling so modest, she unsnapped her shorts and pulled the T-shirt out from the waistband. Then she grabbed the edges of the cotton and got ready to pull. Unfortunately, getting that shirt over her head by herself wasn't going to happen anytime soon. Her ribs were so sore that raising her arms sent waves of pain through her midsection. "Hey, Jarred? I think I need more help than I thought."

Slowly, he turned around.

"I'm having trouble with getting the shirt off." She lifted her arms up a few inches to demonstrate how stuck she was.

As if he were an engineer designing a new bridge or something, Jarred looked at her problem in all seriousness. "I can help with that." Easily, he tucked one arm in an armhole, then the other, and carefully pulled the soft cotton over her head. When the shirt floated to the ground, he held her shoulders and gazed into her eyes. "You okay? Did I hurt you?"

"I'm okay."

"Good. Now we'll just finish up." With the competency of a professional nurse, Jarred helped her stand up, then step out of her khaki shorts.

A few more movements had her bra off and her underwear gone. Before she had a moment to wonder what he was thinking, he wrapped one arm around her waist, the other under her knees…and then deposited her into the tub.

The hot soapy water felt wonderful. The generous amount of suds made her feel almost covered. With a little moan of delight, she leaned back.

His eyes widened. "Pain?"

"Just the opposite. You were right. This does feel good."

After tossing her clothes out of the way, he sat on the stool she'd just vacated. "I'm almost always right," he said smugly. "You should listen to me more often."

His words—and the situation they were in—made her smile. "Maybe I should." Funny how she finally felt her best… when she was carrying a black eye, two broken ribs and a whole slew of bruises and cuts. And funny that in spite of all those injuries, her light heart didn't seem to notice. Not one bit.

Chapter Twenty-Six

The more things changed, the more they stayed the same. That had usually been Serena's mantra, and lately it had never felt more true.

Take everything that had happened since her accident, for example. After Jarred had helped her bathe, they'd watched some TV together. She had some of the soup he'd heated up, while he made do with saltines and peanut butter.

And the tension between them intensified. No matter how hard she tried, Serena hadn't been able to wish away the memories of being in his arms.

Of kissing him in the library.

And, of course, in the barn.

Things must have been on his mind, too, because remarkably early he'd told her good-night and had spent the night on the couch.

Yep, after dancing around the issue of how things were between them—being friends again but friends with good memories—they'd mutually agreed that it would be better if, perhaps, they kept a little more distance.

So, the next morning he'd left, and her sister, Tracy, had taken over nursing duties. Over the next few days, a whole host of other people had stopped by, too, armed with casseroles. Hannah and Paula. Gwen. Mr. Valentine from the restaurant brought over a meal. Even Veronica had come by for a visit, armed with a lovely bouquet of gerbera daisies.

Jarred had come over again, but had brought Ginny, too. Ginny had handed her one of her beloved Penelope books. "We were missing you," he'd said simply.

"I missed y'all, too." So, together, the three of them had curled up on her bed and read about the horse's latest madcap adventures. Before long, Ginny fell asleep.

Then she and Jarred had spent the next hour just catching up. And holding hands.

For a while there, he'd looked as though he had been about to say something, but every time she prodded him, he clammed up.

So she'd let it pass…but she hadn't been happy about it.

Fact was this relationship of theirs was making her half-crazy. They'd gone from friends to lovers to nurse and patient to friends again—all in barely a month's time. And, well, Serena didn't really know how that friendship thing was going to work. Now that she knew what his bare chest felt like beneath her hands.

And now that she knew just how talented he was in the kissing department. Try as she might, she couldn't seem to forget about it all.

So, here she was, waiting on Jarred Riddell again. He had insisted on taking her to the library so she could work for a few hours. Since her car had gone to a junkyard in heaven, she was more than happy to take him up on his offer.

When the clock struck twelve, the doorbell rang.

Opening the door, she couldn't resist teasing him. "Jarred, since when did you become so punctual?"

He grinned, holding up his wrist. "Since someone told me gentlemen wear watches."

She fought to close her mouth. But it was hard, because there, in broad daylight, stood an exceptionally handsome

Jarred Riddell. Though he was clad in his usual uniform of jeans, button-down shirt and boots, all were clean and spiffy-looking. He was freshly shaved. His eyes sparkled under the brim of his white felt Stetson. "You look very handsome," she said.

Eyes shining, he held out a hand. "Ready, Seri?"

"Oh, um. Sure." She grabbed her purse and locked her door. And then took his proffered arm as they slowly walked down the flight of stairs to the parking lot. To her amazement, he shortened his stride to keep pace with her. And opened her door with ease before hopping into the driver's side of his truck.

The minute his door closed, she smelled his cologne.

She eyed him again. "So, you seem awfully dressed up today." Tension knotted her insides as she attempted to figure out the reason why. "Do, ah…you have plans?"

"I do."

Well, she should have expected that, Serena supposed. Jarred had never been the type of man to sit around and do nothing. "With Veronica?"

"No." He glanced her way as he stopped at a streetlight. "I told you she and I didn't suit."

"She told me that, too. Sorry, I don't know why I ask things like that…" Her voice drifted off as an uncomfortable silence began to rise between them. Who was he dating now? She wondered. And wished she didn't care.

When he pulled into the library parking lot, she turned to him and smiled as best she could. "Well, thanks so much for dropping me off."

"Oh, for heaven's sakes. I'm not just dropping you off, Seri. I'm walking in with you, too."

For all his good looks, he sure seemed more irritated with the world than usual. "That's not necessary."

"I think differently. Now sit here while I act like a gentleman."

So she let him walk around and get her door. She took his hand when he held it out. And did her best to push everything she'd ever dreamed about away.

Regrets held no place in her life. She was going to get through things just fine. It was a good thing that she and Jarred were back to being buddies again.

It was just terrific. Friends were hard to come by, and he was one of the best. Definitely.

And, shoot. There was a real good chance that in time— maybe in a year or two—she'd be able to look at Jarred and not think about kissing him.

She'd see his smile and hardly remember when he'd smiled at her in the shower.

One day, she'd see him escort some pretty thing to dinner or to a dance…and she'd almost feel no jealousy.

One day. Yes, one day she was going to feel all those things, for sure.

The main room of the library was a cool, welcome change from the muggy heat outside. But the quiet was startling. Lunch hour was one of their busiest times of the day. "Where is everybody?"

"Hannah closed up for a while."

"What?"

"Don't get all excited. She's going to open back up at two."

"But…that's not allowed."

"So? She did."

"But…what will the patrons think?"

"Most likely that they'll have to come back tomorrow," he said almost too patiently.

Serena examined him again. And noticed that his usual air

of confidence was firmly back into place. Whatever tug-of-war he'd been waging with himself had finally ended.

Now he looked to be firmly in charge again.

She was just curious enough about what had happened to walk forward when he tugged on her hand a bit.

"Seri, come on over here, would you? I want to show you something."

There was a time to argue, and there was a time to follow directions. Serena decided to keep her mouth shut and follow.

Back behind the stacks was a little table, covered in a white tablecloth. Sitting neatly on top were two china place settings, complete with linen napkins and champagne glasses.

It was beautiful.

"Jarred Riddell, what are you up to?"

"I'm having a little graduation ceremony, of course."

"For who?"

"For *whom,* you mean? For me, of course." He opened up a cooler that was off to the side and withdrew a bottle of champagne and two slices of chocolate cake.

He pulled out her chair. "Seri, the truth is, I'm so fancy, I ain't hardly good for regular company no more."

She took her seat and watched him. "Is that right?"

"Mmm-hmm." With a few deft motions, he uncorked the bottle and filled their glasses. As the sparkling wine shimmered in the crystal, he sat down across from her.

Feeling a little at a loss of what to do, she unfolded her napkin and placed it on her lap. And waited.

But not for long.

Looking especially pleased, Jarred picked up one delicate glass and held it up in the air. "Cheers, Serena," he said huskily. "Here's to me."

"Cheers," she echoed, then sipped. As she'd expected, the wine was ice-cold and refreshingly dry. Expensive.

"Now try the cake. I baked it myself."

She almost believed him. Carefully, she took an experimental bite. Instantly, rich, dark chocolate exploded in her mouth. "It's wonderful."

"I thought so."

He looked so smug, she laughed. "This is quite the event. Want to tell me why you picked the library?"

He leaned back in his chair. "There's a couple of reasons. One, I needed someplace to set things up and my house wouldn't do. I swear, it's like Grand Central Station these days."

"And two?"

"We had our lessons here, so it made sense. Plus, well, I like seeing you in the library." His voice lowered, became softer. "Fact is, it makes me happy to see you here."

Her heart started beating a little faster. "And three?"

He sipped his wine again, then set down the glass. "And three…"

She leaned forward. "Yes?"

"I guess I just wanted you to be pleased with me," he murmured as he rested his elbows on the table. Just as she'd taught him not to do.

His blue eyes met hers. "Seri, are you pleased, honey?"

Her mouth had gone dry. "Uh-huh."

"I'm glad. Which brings us to four."

"Four? How many points do you have, Jarred?"

He shook his head slightly, as though he was out of patience with himself. "As many as it takes for me to finally tell you that you're special to me. That you're everything to me."

"Jarred?"

He held up five fingers. "Shoot. I still can't spit it out. What I'm saying is that you've always had my heart, Serena.

I love you. I love you a lot…it's, ah, just taken me a while to remember that it's okay to love. And, well, I'm hoping that one day you'll love me, too."

He loved her? She had his heart? This was the stuff her dreams were made of. She bit her bottom lip. "Do you have any more points to make?"

He looked at her lips for a brief moment then slowly shook his head. "I don't think so. Fact is, I've been so busy laying my heart out to you I forgot to keep count. I love you, Serena, I love you and I want you in my life for good. I want to kiss you in the shower and I want to take you out to dinner. I want to hold your umbrella in the rain, and I want to listen to you read to our children. I want to be able to look at you in the moonlight and have my head wrapped in so many memories of our life together, that even more time with you feels like a gift. So, what do you say, Serena Higgens? Want to be my girl? Forever?"

Her eyes grew damp. "Jarred Riddell, that was almost poetic."

"Oh, yeah?" He looked pleased. Standing up, he walked over to her and held out a hand.

When she took it, he guided her to her feet. He wrapped his arms around her waist and said, "I don't know if you've heard, but I had one heck of a charm-school teacher. She taught me well."

Resting her palms on his chest, she looked up at him. Up at those blue eyes she knew so well. "Is that right?"

"Uh-huh." With care, he leaned down and kissed her tenderly. Taking his time, as if they had a lifetime to kiss and hold each other. "Actually…just about everything I've ever needed to know…I learned from you, Serena Higgens."

"Then, I suppose, my job here is done," she whispered.

Then Jarred kissed her again. Right there in library. Right there in the middle of Electra, Texas.

Where Serena Higgens had always been. Waiting for him.

* * * * *

*Be sure to look for Shelley Galloway's next book,
MY TRUE COWBOY, and find out
who claims Junior's, er, Cal Jr.'s heart!*

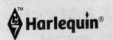

Harlequin®

COMING NEXT MONTH

Available May 10, 2011

#1353 A RANCHER'S PRIDE
American Romance's Men of the West
Barbara White Daille

#1354 THE COWBOY'S TRIPLETS
Callahan Cowboys
Tina Leonard

#1355 SUDDENLY TEXAN
Brody's Crossing
Victoria Chancellor

#1356 THE MARRIAGE SOLUTION
Fatherhood
Megan Kelly

You can find more information on upcoming
Harlequin® titles, free excerpts and more at
www.HarlequinInsideRomance.com.

HARCNM0411

REQUEST YOUR FREE BOOKS!
2 FREE NOVELS PLUS 2 FREE GIFTS!

LOVE, HOME & HAPPINESS

*With an evil force hell-bent on destruction,
two enemies must unite to find a truth that turns
all-too-personal when passions collide.*

*Enjoy a sneak peek in Jenna Kernan's next installment
in her original* TRACKER *series, GHOST STALKER,
available in May, only from Harlequin Nocturne.*

"**W**ho are you?" he snarled.

Jessie lifted her chin. "Your better."

His smile was cold. "Such arrogance could only come from a Niyanoka."

She nodded. "Why are you here?"

"I don't know." He glanced about her room. "I asked the birds to take me to a healer."

"And they have done so. Is that *all* you asked?"

"No. To lead them away from my friends." His eyes fluttered and she saw them roll over white.

Jessie straightened, preparing to flee, but he roused himself and mastered the momentary weakness. His eyes snapped open, locking on her.

Her heart hammered as she inched back.

"Lead who away?" she whispered, suddenly afraid of the answer.

"The ghosts. Nagi sent them to attack me so I would bring them to her."

The wolf must be deranged because Nagi did not send ghosts to attack living creatures. He captured the evil ones after their death if they refused to walk the Way of Souls, forcing them to face judgment.

"Her? The healer you seek is also female?"

"Michaela. She's Niyanoka, like you. The last Seer of Souls and Nagi wants her dead."

Jessie fell back to her seat on the carpet as the possibility of this ricocheted in her brain. Could it be true?

"Why should I believe you?" But she knew why. His black aura, the part that said he had been touched by death. Only a ghost could do that. But it made no sense.

Why would Nagi hunt one of her people and why would a Skinwalker want to protect her? She had been trained from birth to hate the Skinwalkers, to consider them a threat.

His intent blue eyes pinned her. Jessie felt her mouth go dry as she considered the impossible. Could the trickster be speaking the truth? Great Mystery, what evil was this?

She stared in astonishment. There was only one way to find her answers. But she had never even met a Skinwalker before and so did not even know if they dreamed.

But if he dreamed, she would have her chance to learn the truth.

Look for GHOST STALKER by Jenna Kernan,
available May only from Harlequin Nocturne,
wherever books and ebooks are sold.

Harlequin Romance

*Don't miss an irresistible new trilogy
from acclaimed author*

SUSAN MEIER

Greek Tycoons become devoted dads!

Coming in April 2011
The Baby Project

Whitney Ross is terrified when she becomes guardian
to a tiny baby boy, but everything changes when
she meets dashing Darius Andreas, Greek tycoon
and now a brand-new daddy!

Second Chance Baby *(May 2011)*
Baby on the Ranch *(June 2011)*